THE SHADOW SHOOTER

It was so dark now that the man and his horse were almost indistinguishable. Madigan never heard the first rifle shot. He only knew that it had been fired by the bright flash. Before he could jerk the reins, the rifle spat flame a second time. Madigan tried to saw the reins now, to turn the roan, but the big horse lost its stride for a second. Then something snapped, and the horse went down and something ripped through the sleeve of his shirt, and Madigan knew he'd been hit as he sailed headlong over the roan and landed hard on his side.

He tried to get to his feet, but the wind was knocked out of him. He rolled over, gasping and clawing for his pistol and not finding it. The rifleman ran forward then stopped. He turned his back just as the lightning flashed. Madigan saw nothing more than the shirt and jeans of a drenched cowboy, the holster on his hip and the rifle in his hand.

By Bill Dugan

Duel on the Mesa
Texas Drive
Gun Play at Cross Creek
Brady's Law
Death Song
Madigan's Luck

War Chiefs

Geronimo
Chief Joseph
Crazy Horse
Quanah Parker
Sitting Bull

Published by HarperPaperbacks

ATTENTION: ORGANIZATIONS AND CORPORATIONS

Most HarperPaperbacks are available at special quantity discounts for bulk purchases for sales promotions, premiums, or fund-raising. For information, please call or write:
Special Markets Department, HarperCollins Publishers,
10 East 53rd Street, New York, N.Y. 10022.
Telephone: (212) 207-7528. Fax: (212) 207-7222.

MADIGAN'S LUCK

BILL DUGAN

HarperPaperbacks
A Division of HarperCollinsPublishers

This is a work of fiction. The characters, incidents, and dialogues are products of the author's imagination and are not to be construed as real. Any resemblance to actual events or persons, living or dead, is entirely coincidental.

Ha perPaperbacks   *A Division of* HarperCollins*Publishers*
10 East 53rd Street, New York, N.Y. 10022

Cover illustration by Tony Gabriele

First printing: December 1994

Printed in the United States of America

HarperPaperbacks and colophon are trademarks of HarperCollins*Publishers*

❖ 10 9 8 7 6 5 4 3 2 1

D ave Madigan finished his coffee, then wiped his mouth on his sleeve. He knew it was a mistake even before he was finished, and he glanced at his wife, Sarah, hoping she hadn't noticed. She had.

"Sorry," he said.

She gave him a crooked grin. "It'd be all right if I didn't have something else to do, David. I swear, there are times when I think you have no manners at all. And other times when I *know* you haven't."

She laughed, and he walked over to kiss her on the top of the head. "I guess I deserved that."

"Of course you did. But I don't suppose you'll ever learn, so I guess I might as well get used to it." She stood on tip-toe to peck him on the nose. "You coming back for lunch?"

He shook his head. "Nope. I'll be up in the hills till pretty near sundown. If I'm going to make the deadline for that army contract, I got to get at least fifty head together by Friday. That only gives me three or four days. Working alone, that isn't much time."

"I still don't see why you don't hire somebody to help you. I don't mean permanently, but at least until you get the horses together."

Madigan sighed. "I wish to hell I could afford to do that. But I can't. We got a bank payment the end of the month, and as it is, even if I meet the deadline, I don't know if I'll have payment on the horses by then. If I don't, we'll be in big trouble."

"Mr. Cartwright will give you an extension. He always does."

"Lou Cartwright is a banker, and he'll do what bankers always do. He'll do what's best for the bank. If that means letting a little fish like me go belly up, then that's what he'll do. You know that as well as I do, Sarah."

"You're so pessimistic, David. Sometimes I think you expect bad luck so much you kind of bring it on yourself."

"Bad luck does seem to find me pretty easily, doesn't it?" He grinned, even though he didn't really feel like it. But there wasn't time to get into a discussion, and it was easier to go along with Sarah than try to change her mind. Besides, he did enough worrying for the two of them. No need to make her miserable, too.

He looked at her, wondering that, at thirty-five, she still looked as trim as she did. Not like some of the women in Clarion, who looked worn out, used up somehow. Her mass of auburn curls was as bright as her smile, and her green eyes still sparkled with mischief. Under the freckles, her skin was still smooth as silk.

He wished he had fared as well. Only three years older, he felt sometimes as if age, or maybe just worry, was wearing him down. His hair was still black, his blue eyes still managed to charm her out of an occasional fit of anger. But under the sunburned skin, something was diminishing him, slowly but surely, like a grinding wheel slowly wearing away the blade under the pretense of keeping it sharp, and he thought he would one day end up like his father, a bag of old bones under sagging, mottled skin. If he lived that long.

He walked out to the corral, where his horse was already saddled. He swung up into the saddle, jerked the reins a bit, and walked the big roan stallion across the yard. As he passed the house, he could see Sarah inside, sitting in her rocker, a pile of sewing in her lap. Even through the screen, he could see the peculiar way she pursed her lips when she sewed. He always teased her about it, telling her that it looked as if she was afraid the needle was deadly poison.

As hard as he worked, he knew she worked

just as hard, and although he wished her life were easier, he didn't know any other way for either of them. They were hanging on by their fingernails, and there were times when he didn't think they'd make it through the month.

As he moved away from the house, he thought about what Sarah had said, wondering whether maybe there might be something to it. He wasn't sure whether he was as unlucky as all that, but it sure seemed like it sometimes. But he knew that thinking happy thoughts didn't pay the bills, and he didn't know how else to deal with things he couldn't control except to worry about them. His father had been a worrier, too, and it had probably killed him. But when the choice was between dying of worry or overwork, it was no choice at all. Deep down, he believed Sarah understood that, or at least he hoped so.

He was running nearly five hundred head of horses, all good stock, all branded, but they were on the open range and, without help, rounding up fifty horses and getting them nearly a hundred miles to Fort Peterson was not a sure thing. He would be lucky to make it, because the purchasing officer at the fort, a persnickety major from Boston, who looked down his nose at anyone who lacked a Harvard education, was as unforgiving a man as he'd ever met. The contract said fifty horses by noon on Friday the 23rd, and according to Major Harrison Fletcher, that didn't mean 12:01, and it sure as hell didn't mean Saturday the 24th, no matter what time of day.

Most purchasing officers were realists. They knew that horses had minds of their own, and they were willing to be flexible, as long as it didn't penalize the post or its men. But Fletcher was such a bastard, Madigan knew that if he showed up at ten after noon on Friday with sixty horses, Fletcher would void the deal and put the contract out for re-bid. It was stupid, but it was by the book, and that was all that mattered to the major. It also meant that Madigan would not be eligible to bid on another contract for six months. And if that happened, then he might just as well put a torch to the barn because without the army contracts, he would go under in six weeks, let alone months.

The sky began to darken as he rode into the hills, and a nervous glance at the clouds told him that he was in for wet weather. As if he didn't have enough trouble already. But he had no choice, so he kicked the roan and pushed it a little harder, leaning slightly forward in the saddle, as if that would get him where he was going any sooner.

Up ahead, the stands of lodgepole and pinyon looked dark against the horizon. He could see some of his stock grazing on the next ridge, smudges of brown, white, and gray against the trees behind them. He had a decision to make, and he didn't know which way to go. He could rig a makeshift corral, and drive all fifty head in once he rounded them up, or he could make several trips, driving smaller groups as he found them back to the main corral. The second way was probably safer, because he could spot the leader of a small herd, get a rope on him, and the rest of the horses would follow him in. If he gathered all the animals at once, he ran the risk of the herd leaders fighting among themselves, or scattering the herd on the way back. Working by himself, either way had its drawbacks.

"Old son," he whispered, "you ain't gonna get nothing done at all, unless you make up your mind. What's it gonna be?"

And he decided to take the safe way. It would take more time, but in the long run, it was better. He hated the idea of spending all day rounding up fifty head only to have them scatter to the four winds as soon as he tried to move them down to the corral.

His mind made up, he reached into his saddlebags and grabbed his field glasses. The scuffed leather, barely carrying a trace of the gold lettering that had once identified them as property of the U.S. Army, felt dry and brittle under his fingers. He looked at the glasses, shaking his head. The crumbling leather seemed like a metaphor for the precarious state of his finances. It was perfect, in fact, almost too perfect.

Training the glasses on the next ridge, he counted heads, and nodded appreciatively when he got to eighteen. Not a bad start, better than a third of the total he needed. He found the leader, a prickly black that had once taken a swipe at him with its front hooves when he'd come too close. It was a spirited stallion, and he knew it was going to be tough to get a rope on him. Holding him would be another thing, too, he thought.

But he nudged his horse into a trot and angled down across the slope, listening to the swish of the tall grass against the roan's legs. Checking the sky again, he saw the sun slip behind a cloud for a few seconds, then reappear, but much dimmed. A haze was trailing behind the cloud, and the sun looked suddenly pale. Huge masses of black cumulus clouds tumbled out of the Rocky Mountains like coal down a chute.

He could feel the wind pick up, and saw the grass ahead of him turn from bright green to gray as it bent before the gusts. Far across the valley, he saw the first flash of lightning, and clenched his ears against the almost immediate clap of thunder. It started with the sound of cloth tearing, as if the sky were made of denim clenched in two giant fists ripping it asunder, then finished with a terrible explosion.

The roan was getting nervous, and Madigan himself wasn't all that thrilled to be out in the open on the hillside. He knew enough not to take cover under trees, especially tall ones, but he wasn't about to get off the roan and lie down, either. If lightning hit him, that would just prove to Sarah that he was right to expect bad luck.

Still, he pushed the roan even harder, the fast trot pounding the ground beneath the lush grass with the sound of muffled drums. When he reached the creek that bisected the valley floor into almost perfect halves, he waded the roan across the water and started up the far side.

He could see the horses without the glasses, but just barely. He wanted to get close before they lost themselves in the trees. When he neared the crest, they were half a mile to the east moving along at an easy lope, the big black leading them along the ridgeline. The pines were off to the left, where the land sloped downward a bit into a shallow bowl, then swept up even higher.

He was closing on them patiently, not wanting to spook them, but not wanting to wait too long, either. Another lightning flash turned everything vivid for a moment, almost bleaching color out of the grass and the horses themselves. And when the glare faded, it seemed even darker. He felt the first few drops of rain spatter his Stetson, and one cold drop hit the back of his right hand with a loud slap. It felt like a spent minié ball, it hit so hard.

A quarter of a mile separated him from the horses now, and he looked up again, just as a man on horseback moved out of the trees and fell in right behind the horses. Madigan heard a loud yip, and the horses took off, the mysterious rider right behind them, waving his hat in his right hand. His voice barely carried on the rising wind, but enough that Madigan could hear the "yip-yip-geeyah," almost in time to the flapping hat.

Madigan put the spurs to the roan now, trying to keep up. He didn't know whether the rider had seen him or not, but it sure as hell didn't look like it. Only a damned fool would try to run off a man's horses right under his nose, so it was almost certain the rider hadn't noticed him.

The horses were running hard now, the rider right on their tails. Madigan shouted, but the rider gave no notice. The wind was really picking up now, and it had begun to rain still harder. Glancing for a moment at the sky, Madigan knew it was going to be a hell of a storm, and that it wouldn't hold off its full fury for more than ten or fifteen minutes. That didn't give him very much time to get the rider's attention. Or to decide what he'd do once he managed to get it.

Not knowing what else to do, Madigan pulled his Colt and aimed it behind him, squeezing the trigger. He heard the sharp crack, then heard it echo from the opposite hill and come bouncing back from the tree-covered slope a split second later. The rider turned then, and for a second Madigan thought he was going to slow down, but then he reached to his right hip and a second later a spurt of flame licked out at Madigan.

The sonofabitch is shooting at me! Madigan thought. *What the hell is wrong with him?*

Dropping low on the back of the roan, trying to keep his profile as small as possible, he hugged the horse's neck and kicked him with the spurs gain. He didn't like using spurs, especially on a good horse, and the roan was the best he'd ever had, but there were times when it was necessary, and this sure as hell seemed like one.

The rider fired again, this time aiming at the sky, and the muzzle flash was answered almost instantly by another bolt of lightning. Once more the sky sounded as if it were being torn in half, and now the rain really cut loose. Madigan was soaked to the skin in thirty seconds. He was closing on the horse thief, because that's how he'd begun to think of him, but not fast enough to suit him. He flapped his knees, and whispered to the roan to go even harder.

He was only two hundred yards behind the rider now, and still closing, although more slowly, and suddenly the rider reined in. Madigan thought maybe he was going to give up, and half expected to see the horseman turn and cut for the trees. Instead, he dismounted. At a hundred and fifty yards, Madigan started to ease up, then saw the man yank a rifle from a boot, and drop to one knee. Through the slashing rain, it was hard to see clearly, and what he was seeing was so hard to believe, he still wasn't sure it was happening.

It was so dark now that the man and his horse were almost indistinguishable, even though they were little more than a hundred yards away. Madigan never heard the first rifle shot, only knew by the bright flash that it had been fired. Before he could jerk the reins, the rifle spat flame a second time. Madigan tried to saw the reins now, to turn the roan, and the big horse lost its stride for a second. Then something snapped, and he wasn't sure whether it was bone breaking or not, but the horse went down and something ripped through the sleeve of his shirt, and he knew he'd been hit as he sailed headlong over the roan and landed hard on his side.

He tried to get to his feet, but the wind was knocked out of him, and he rolled over, gasping and clawing for his pistol and not finding it. The rifleman ran forward three or four steps then stopped. He turned his back just as the lightning flashed again, but Madigan saw nothing more than the shirt and jeans of a drenched cowboy, the holster on his hip, and the rifle in his hand.

The man climbed into the saddle again, turned and fired the rifle once more, this time one-handed, and by the time the lightning flashed again, he was just a shadow vanishing over the hilltop, hard on the heels of a dozen of Madigan's best horses.

2

Madigan watched as the gunman disappeared over the hill, a dozen head of horses gone with him. He got to his feet, clutching his arm to keep the bleeding down. The rain continued to hammer at him, slashing in translucent sheets on the stiff wind. He was soaked, he was bleeding, and he was madder than hell, but there wasn't a goddamn thing he could do about any of it for the moment.

Tugging a handkerchief from his pocket, he held it in his teeth and rolled up his right sleeve until he could see the gunshot wound. It was an ugly furrow, but it wasn't deep enough to have struck bone. The rain made it sting, and he shook the arm, ignoring the pain, until some of the water had been shaken loose. Then he wrapped the handkerchief twice around the three-inch gully, and, using his teeth to hold one end, managed to fashion a clumsy knot with his free hand.

Then, rolling up the other sleeve, he turned to look at his horse. The big roan lay on its side. It quivered, and tried to raise its head as he approached, but the bullet had broken a leg bone, and there was no way to save the horse. Cursing as much at himself as at the gunman, he shook his head and reached for his Colt. When he felt the empty holster, he remembered the spill he'd taken and started looking around him. The grass was thick, and he didn't see the gun anywhere.

His rifle was three hundred yards away, and he had a better chance of finding the pistol, so he started kicking at the grass in widening circles around the horse. A flash of lightning revealed the bone grip in the tall grass, and he bent over to retrieve the gun as the thunder exploded overhead.

The horse gave a pitiful nicker, and he turned to see it trying to get up. But the broken leg was useless, and the roan lay down again, raising its head to watch him as he approached. Madigan bent over to loosen the cinch, then coaxed the saddle from the roan, and took his slicker from his saddlebags. Leaving a coil of rope to one side, he wrapped the slicker around the saddle and the rest of his gear to keep it from getting any wetter than it already was.

He knew why he was doing it. He was trying

to avoid doing what he knew he had no choice but to do. He took a deep breath, glanced through the slashing rain once more at the crest of the ridge where the gunman had ridden out of sight, then sighed. Walking back to the horse to stand over the roan's head, he thumbed the Colt's hammer back, aimed the pistol, and squeezed the trigger. The hammer clicked on a dud round, prolonging the agony, and he cursed aloud, tilting his head back and yelling at the sky as if it, or something beyond it, were responsible.

Once more he thumbed the hammer back, aimed, and squeezed. This time, the gun fired, and he heard the sharp crack of the bullet breaking the roan's skull. The horse quivered once more, its legs jerking in one final spasm, then it gave a great sigh, like an old man drifting off to sleep, and lay still.

"Damn you!" Madigan whispered. "God damn you to hell!" He clenched his fist and shook it at the ridge line, suddenly outlined once more against the sky by another lightning flash. This time, instead of the sudden rumble, the thunder was a muted mutter.

The wind howled through the trees, and he could hear the rain slashing among the crowns of the lodgepoles, hissing the way snow did when it lashed the sides of the house during winter storms. His arm ached, and a small trickle of watery blood still veined his forearm, and he smeared it with his fingertips, wiping them on his jeans.

"Time to go," he said. Then, like someone

who wasn't sure he'd been heard, he said it again, this time louder. "Time to go." He bent down to pat the roan on its lifeless flank as he moved past, almost crying now, half with sorrow and half with helpless rage.

Walking to the mound of gear, he snatched up the coil of rope. It was a long walk home, and he thought that some of the scattered horses would be close enough for him to maybe get a rope on one. Most of them weren't broken, but a few of them were fairly docile, and if his luck took a sudden turn for the better, he might be able to spare himself the walk. But it had been a long time since he'd seen a rainbow or found a four-leaf clover, so he wasn't expecting much.

And his luck held. Except for retrieving his Winchester, it was all bad. It continued to rain. The wind whipped at him, driving the cold rain into his face half the time, then teasing him as it seemed to subside a bit only to pick up steam again and renew its attack. His clothes were drenched, his boots full of water and sloshing with every step. One hip was killing him from the spill, and he knew it was badly bruised. But he kept walking because he had no choice. It took him more than two hours to reach the last hill before the house, and by the time he reached the crest, his legs felt as if they were made of lead.

He could see a light in the window, and the column of smoke from the chimney made him think of heat and food. He started downhill with renewed energy that lasted about fifteen steps, until his exhaustion reasserted itself, and he slogged the rest of the way to the bottom of the hill. He stopped at the barn just long enough to drop off the rope, then squished through the mud to the front porch.

Sarah heard him climb the steps and came to the door. When she saw him, she started to laugh. "You look like a drowned rat," she said. But something in his response stopped her. "What's wrong, David? What happened?" She pushed open the screen to step out onto the porch.

Spotting the bloody handkerchief knotted around his arm, she raised one hand to her mouth. "I'm all right," he said. "Just a scratch."

"A scratch, how . . . what happened?"

He shook his head. "Not now, Sarah. Not now. Let me change clothes first."

She looked past him then, and must have realized that his horse wasn't at the hitching rail. "Did you walk home?"

He nodded. "Yeah. I walked. I walked every goddamned yard of the way." He yanked open the screen door and stepped inside, Sarah following him in.

"David . . . ?"

He took a deep breath. "Somebody was running off some of our stock. I spotted him, and I chased him, but he got away with about a dozen horses."

She knew there was more to it than that. "What happened to your arm? Where's your horse?"

And he dropped wearily into a chair and told

her the rest of it. He watched her face the whole time, trying to read her mind, but her expression kept changing from sentence to sentence, as if she didn't know what to think, and by the time he was finished, she was on the verge of tears. "You could have been killed."

He nodded. "I guess so, yeah."

She knelt beside the chair. "Let me look at that arm. Before he could answer, her fingers fumbled at the knot. Soaked by the rain, the knot was swollen, and it fought her for several seconds. When it finally came loose, she let the ends fall, then slowly unwrapped it.

"At least it's not likely to be stuck to the wound," he said.

But she removed it carefully, chewing on her lower lip, her expression so intent, it looked almost as if she could feel the pain herself. And when she finally had the handkerchief loose, she stuck her tongue out and dabbed at the blood with one corner of the sopping cloth. "We'll have to clean it out," she said. "Then I think you should go to town and see Doctor Clemmons."

"I'm going to town, all right, but it isn't for Doc Clemmons. I want to talk to Matt Fisher. Somebody rustled a dozen of our horses, and I want the sonofabitch, in jail. Whoever he is . . . "

"Why don't you change into some dry clothes, while I heat some water. We'll clean that wound, put some salve on it, and you can have Doctor Clemmons look at it. I don't think you need stitches, but . . . "

She got up and grabbed a pot, poured it half full of water, and hung it over the fire to heat. Madigan got wearily to his feet and went into the bedroom. Stripping off his clothes, he dropped them in a sodden heap and fell back on the bed, bone weary and tired, too, of always swimming upstream.

He was nearly asleep by the time Sarah came in with the pot of water and several towels. She knelt beside the bed, and he gave her a weak smile, then closed his eyes again. Her fingers rested on the swollen and discolored hip, and he winced. "That's an ugly bruise, mister. You're lucky nothing's broken."

He groaned agreement, and lay there like a dead man while she cleaned the wound. It hurt like hell, but he was too tired to protest. It was easier to just lie still and endure the sting of the water in the wound, and the burning of the hot towel. He heard the pop of a metal lid, then smelled the fumes of an ointment, the camphor swirling around him as her movements fanned it toward him. Lifting the arm, she bound it in gauze, then wrapped it and tied it off. "That ought to hold you until Doctor Clemmons has a chance to see it."

He felt the bed shift as she sat beside him, then smelled her hair as she leaned over him and began to dry him off. "You're black and blue all over," she said. "That must have been quite a spill."

He nodded, opened his eyes, and reached up with one arm to wrap it around her. He pulled her down beside him, nestled his face in her hair, and mumbled, "This won't stop us, Sarah. I'll make that contract. Don't worry."

"I won't," she whispered. "I know we'll be all right." She turned to kiss him on the forehead, then extricated herself from the arm he'd draped across her shoulders and sat up. "I'm going to heat up some soup. Why don't you sleep for awhile, honey?"

He shook his head. "Can't. Got to talk to Sheriff Fisher. Whoever that sonofabitch is, he's got a dozen head of prime stock, and I want it back. The longer I wait, the more likely it is he'll get clean away."

"He's already gotten away, David. If the sheriff is going to find him, he can start looking for him tomorrow. Go in the morning."

He shook his head again, this time more vehemently. "Not a chance." He sat up then, and dropped his legs to the floor beside her. "I'll take you up on that soup, but I'm going to town right afterward."

She stood up and he patted her rump, then let his hand rest on her right hip. "I'll be fine, Sarah. Don't worry about me."

She took a deep breath and her body tensed under his hand. He thought she was going to argue, but she let her breath out softly and nodded. "All right. Let me heat up your supper." She started to move, but he curled his fingers into the fabric of her dress and tugged her back. "I mean it, Sarah. It'll be fine."

She went to the front of the cabin, and he dressed in dry clothes, then gathered the sodden mess he had been wearing, carried it out to the wicker hamper in the front, and dropped it with a dull thud.

Sarah set a place for him and poured him a cup of hot coffee. He sipped the coffee until the soup was ready. When Sarah filled his bowl, he spooned the soup down, then wiped the bowl with a hunk of bread. Smacking his lips, he got to his feet. "That turned the trick. Hell, the way I feel, you'd never know I'd been shot at and hit, then thrown from a horse all in one day," he said.

She looked at him sharply. "David, don't make light of it. You could have been killed."

"The man couldn't hit the side of a barn at fifty feet, hon."

"He hit you, didn't he?"

"Lucky shot."

"His luck or yours, David?"

Madigan smiled. "I believe it was my luck that he hit me, otherwise the bullet never would have come within a mile of me."

He slipped on a leather jacket and walked to the window. "Looks like the rain's just about stopped. At least I won't have to swim into Clarion." He walked over to her where she was bent over the fire and circled her waist with his arms, bumping the bandaged wound, and biting his lip to avoid crying out. "I'll be back as soon as I can."

Inside the circle of his arms, she turned to

face him, and held on tight. "You be careful, David."

"Always am, darlin', always am." He let go of her, then pulled her hands free of his shoulders and went out to the barn. He had to use an old saddle and blanket, and lugged it to the corral, where he picked out a sorrel he'd been hoping to sell, saddled the young stallion, and led it to the rail in front of the porch. He went back inside for his rifle, checked it to make sure it wasn't fouled with mud, and borrowed a towel to wipe it down, then went back outside.

Booting the Winchester, he unhitched the reins and swung into the saddle. He was still tired, but he was also determined, and he set his jaw as he turned the new mount and headed for Clarion.

3

As Madigan rode toward Clarion, the sun finally broke through the clouds. It was late afternoon, and the sun was already beginning to slide toward the horizon, so its sudden appearance was spectacular. Spears of brilliant light stabbed in every direction, and the cloud directly in front of the sun seemed to dissolve, as if it were burning away. The black became gray, then purple, and finally dissipated in a red froth that was there for a moment then gone, leaving the orange ball dominant again.

Far to the east, across the territorial line that separated Colorado from Kansas, Madigan could still see black clouds and flashes of lightning. The shadows of the clouds raced across the rolling hills, turning the grass dark for an instant as they passed, then the grass seemed to glow a fiery green. The road was muddy, water running in the ruts carved by wagon wheels like twin creeks.

His arm hurt now, a dull ache punctuated by an occasional throb as he twisted his wrist or bent his elbow. He let it lie on his thigh, trying to keep it motionless. And his hip was beginning to stiffen up. He had seen the mass of bruises on his chest and legs, and wondered that he hadn't broken a bone. So he supposed that he just might be luckier than he thought.

A mile outside of Clarion, he caught up to a wagon, rocking in the ruts. As he drew close, he could hear the creak of the wagon bed, and the sucking sound of the wheels churning through the mud. He moved off the narrow road and into the grass to move past. The wagon's wheels were slipping as much as they were spinning, and the wooden spokes were clotted with mud, making them heavy, giving the two-horse team all it could handle.

As he moved alongside, he nodded to the driver, a man he didn't recognize, and veered back into the road as soon as he was far enough ahead. Moving up a slight hill, he urged the sorrel on. He was getting anxious to talk to the sheriff, afraid his anger, already beginning to cool, might vanish altogether. Pleasant by nature, he was not a man who relished confrontation, but, distasteful as it might be, he had no choice but to talk to Fisher and tell him what had happened.

He knew it was going to be difficult, if not impossible, to find the man who had stolen the horses. Only a fool would be likely to keep the animals in the vicinity of Clarion. They were branded, and while it was common practice to doctor brands, it wasn't that easy to keep secret. Whoever had stolen the horses was probably long gone, headed someplace where he could do the doctoring without fear of discovery, and sell the horses off quickly. Unlike livestock, money didn't have a brand, and if it was in your pocket, it was yours.

Clarion was on the other side of the hill, and when he broke over the ridge, he relaxed a little, letting the horse find its own pace on the way down. The road snaked back and forth across the long slope in a series of switchbacks. He kept his eyes on the town, its whitewashed buildings so bright they looked almost ghostly in the aftermath of the rain. On the hill on the far side of town, some of the more substantial citizens had their homes, some brick and some frame, and their windows caught the sun and flashed like heliographs as his perspective kept changing.

Even from his vantage point halfway down, he could see the huge puddles in the streets. The sun reflected off one particularly large pool, and the angle made it seem transparent, as if it were a hole in the earth, looking through to sky on the other side of the world. The surface of the pool was blue and white, smeared with orange. He knew, though, that when he got close, it would look considerably less attractive, brown with mud and flecked with bits of straw. That seemed always to be the way things were. From a distance, you thought they were just about perfect, but when you got up close, you saw all the flaws, and wondered how you could have been so gullible.

Sarah always told him it was better to stay optimistic, don't get too close if it meant losing the sense of wonder. But Madigan was too hardheaded for that. He wasn't a dreamer, just a man willing to work hard, and hope a little, for something he wanted. It was ordinary maybe, but that's what he was, an ordinary man, willing to pay his own way. He didn't need help, and wouldn't take it unless he did. The point of living, as Dave Madigan saw it, was not to need help. That's how you measured success. It wasn't your bank account or the size of your house, it was just knowing that whatever you had you'd earned. And you took care of it yourself.

That self-reliance was being challenged now, but there was nothing he could do about it. If he took off after the horse thief on his own, he'd never make the contract deadline. And he couldn't survive without the money it would bring him. But if he just wrote off the loss, then he'd be giving someone an open invitation to come back any damn time he chose and cut out another dozen head. He couldn't survive that way, either.

The more he thought about the stolen horses, the madder he got. And by the time he reached the flats at the bottom of the hill, he was back to the boiling point.

He spurred the sorrel now, and headed down the center of the main street, not bothering to avoid the puddles, since they would soak some of the mud off the horse's hooves. The sheriff's office was at the far end of the street, and when he reached it, he reined in and dismounted, tying the sorrel to the rail. Up the block, he saw Dan Flannery, a rancher he knew, come out of the grocer's and drop a couple of heavy bags into the back of his wagon.

Flannery waved, and Madigan returned the greeting.

"Dave, how are you?" Flannery called, starting toward him. Madigan was torn between the desire to be neighborly and the mission that had brought him to town, but he walked up the street and met Flannery halfway.

The rancher was tall and awkward, his skin more sallow than sunburned. He looked like a collection of sticks assembled into a scarecrow without regard for geometry. His blue eyes were pale, almost watery, and more often than not red-rimmed, evidence of his devotion to whiskey.

Madigan grasped Flannery's extended hand, forgetting the wound in his arm, and winced when they shook hands. Flannery knit his brow and looked puzzled. "You all right, Dave?"

Madigan nodded. "Little scratch on my arm is all."

He held up the injured arm, but his shirt sleeve covered the injury and Flannery still looked mystified. "Thought for a minute there that I didn't know my own strength." He laughed, but Madigan waved off the suggestion.

"That'll be the day. You're about the scrawniest damn Irishman I ever saw, Dan."

For the insult, Flannery feinted a blow to his midsection, then laughed. "So what did happen? You run into Sarah's scissors, or something?"

"I wish it was that simple. Somebody took a shot at me this morning."

"What?"

Madigan told him about the horse thief, and Flannery listened, shaking his head every now and then, but not interrupting. When Madigan was finished, Flannery smacked his brow dramatically. "Damn. You know, I lost a few beeves the last few months. Didn't think much of it, you know, because cows ain't too smart. They wander off, the wolves get 'em, sometimes they just plain get lost. Now you got me thinkin' maybe I been too casual about it."

Madigan shrugged. "Maybe. You ever find a carcass?"

Flannery shook his head. "Nope. Didn't think much of it, though. Like I say, sometimes they just plain wander off. But maybe somebody's been culling a head or two here and there. What're you going to do about the horses?"

"I was just on my way to see Matt Fisher. Figured I better let him know about it."

Flannery grunted. "Matt Fisher couldn't find his ass with both hands. You sure don't think he's gonna waste any time lookin' for some horse thief that's got a day's head start on him, do you?"

"I don't know. That's his job, isn't it?"

"I'm not sure what his job is. And I think I got a better idea than he does." Flannery draped an arm around Madigan's shoulders. "Come on, let's go see if we can build a fire under him."

"No need for you to get involved, Dan."

Flannery looked offended. "The hell there ain't. If somebody's pinchin' horses, maybe he's pinchin' cows, too. Come on." He urged Madigan forward with the press of his arm, and they fell into lockstep, heading back toward the sheriff's office.

Matt Fisher was sitting at his desk. He was reading something and leaned so far forward, his ruddy face was all but buried in a sheaf of papers. He looked up as they entered. "Be with you in a minute, fellas," he said, then went back to his reading, fiddling with a sparse brown mustache with his chubby fingers, round as sausage links.

Madigan pulled up a rickety chair and sat down, while Flannery paced back and forth. It seemed odd how agitated Flannery was, almost as if it were he and not Madigan who had incurred the loss that morning. But Madigan knew Flannery was cursed with a short fuse, and tried to pay no attention to the increasingly loud scrape of boots on the wooden floor.

Finally, the sheriff let the papers drop to the desk top and looked up. "What can I do for you men?" he asked, folding his chubby hands across a solid paunch.

Madigan opened his mouth to explain, but

Flannery seized the opening. "Somebody tried to kill Dave this morning," he said. "Took a shot at him. Hit him in the arm, too."

Fisher nodded, then leaned back in his chair. "Then why don't you let Dave tell me about it, Dan? I expect he knows a little more about it than you do. Unless, of course, it was you did the shooting." He looked intently at Flannery. "It wasn't was it?"

"Of course not!" Flannery spluttered. "Jesus! Next you'll be after sayin' it was me who killed Lincoln."

Once more, Fisher stared intently. "I never did believe Booth done it. You didn't do it, did you, Dan? Shoot Lincoln, I mean?"

And he laughed, but Flannery was not amused. He muttered to himself and snatched another chair from its place by the wall. He looked at Madigan then. "Go on, Dave, tell him."

Madigan cleared his throat. "Not much to tell, really. I was up in the hills, trying to round up some stock, and I spotted somebody running off with about a dozen of my horses. I lit out after him, but he spotted me before I could get too close. I chased him, we exchanged a few shots, and he winged me. Another shot broke my horse's leg, and that was all she wrote."

"You know who it was?"

Madigan shook his head. "Nope. Never did get close enough to get a clear look at him. It was raining to beat the band."

"This the first time you lost horses?"

"Far as I know. They run free up there, Matt. You know that. I don't do a head count."

Flannery butted in. "I been missing a few beeves, too. Probably the same man."

Fisher looked skeptical. "What makes you think so? You see somebody run them off?"

Flannery was annoyed, and his voice was sharp when he answered. "Hell no, I didn't see nobody. I did, I'da put a bullet through him, for sure."

"How come you never said anything to me about it, Dan?" Fisher asked. "First I've heard of it."

"I didn't think nothing of it, until Dave told me about somebody rustling his horses. I just put two and two together then, and . . . "

"Maybe come up with five," Fisher suggested.

"What the hell's that supposed to mean?" Flannery demanded.

Madigan chuckled. "I think what Matt means is that maybe there's no connection. It's probably just a coincidence. You told me you weren't even sure the cows had been stolen."

"That right, Dan?" Fisher asked.

Flannery looked unhappy, but admitted it. "Well, yeah, but now I think maybe there is a connection. I mean, hell, a man who would steal a horse would steal a cow, and vice versa, am I right?"

"You could be, Dan." Fisher agreed. "But then again, it could just be that nobody stole your beeves. Maybe they just run off. Maybe a wolf . . . "

"I been through all that with Dave. I know

all that. I'm just sayin' that maybe there's a connection, is all. And if there is, we got to find whoever done it."

"I'll see what I can do."

"I know what you can do," Flannery snapped. "You can get off your lazy ass and get this thievin' sonofabitch, and clap him in jail. That's what you can do."

"Sure," Fisher said. "I can do that. But first, I got to know who it is. Then I got to find him." He stared at Flannery, daring him to argue with his logic, and when Flannery remained silent, he turned to Madigan.

"You gonna be around tomorrow?"

"I'll be out rounding up some more horses. I got a contract to meet, and not much time to do it."

"That's all right," Fisher said. "You got to be up in the hills anyhow, then, so I'll meet you there, see if I can find anything that might give me a line on who it was. I'll be by around eight or so, if that's all right. By the time I get up there tonight, it'd be dark, so . . . "

"What about my cows, Sheriff?" Flannery demanded.

Fisher nodded. "Don't worry about it. I'll look into it."

"Damn well better, is all I got to say."

Fisher glared at him. "I sure as hell wish it *was* all you got to say, Dan. But I know better." He stood up and extended a hand to Madigan. "See you tomorrow, Dave."

4

The heat was gone. The rain had cooled things down and now, the stars out, the sun long since set, Madigan sat on the front porch, rocking his aching bones in a chair brought all the way from Pennsylvania.

Sarah was inside, finishing up some sewing. He could hear her humming, her rich voice, nearly a contralto, slightly rough around the edges. Trained in a convent school, she sight-read music, and played the piano, too, but they no longer had one. On the long trip from St. Louis, the old spinet had tumbled from the back of the wagon, landed with a crunch of splintering wood and the pop and ping of one parting string after another.

Sarah had been inconsolable for weeks afterward, mourning the dead piano like other women mourned for dead children. He wanted her to have another, but it was expensive, too expensive for now, and although she understood, it was like a tiny fence between them, this loss, one they walked around or stepped over, one that didn't stop them, but one they could never quite forget.

One day, he thought, one day, I'll hear her play again, just like she used to. He edged the chair a little closer to the open door to listen to the music. He thought he recognized the tune, something religious, a hymn, perhaps, or maybe something from that Italian composer she liked so much, Palestrina.

Madigan closed his eyes and rocked quietly, the porch boards creaking the least little bit with every back and forth of the chair. For a little while, he was able to put his worries out of his mind. There was nothing he could do until morning, anyway, and so he told himself that he might just as well relax.

When Sarah stopped singing, he opened his eyes again. He heard the screen-door hinges creak, and tilted his head so that he could see the door. She was standing there, the door held open with one hand, backlit by the lamp. "Want company?" she asked.

He nodded, and resumed rocking. There was a two-seater porch swing suspended from chains bolted into the roof rafters, and she sat down, pushed off, and added the tortured squeal of the chain links to the less insistent squeak of the boards.

"What did the sheriff say?" she asked.

"About what I thought he'd say."

"Which was . . . ?"

"Which was that he'd come out tomorrow, take a look around, and see if there was anything that might help him find the horse thief. He didn't say it, but I got the sense that if he didn't find anything right away, he wasn't going to do too much looking."

"Matthew is a good man. I think he's unfairly maligned. So many of the ranchers and farmers around here think he should be able to find a needle in a haystack, and when he doesn't, they get mad at him, never mind that they don't even know where to find the haystack themselves."

"I don't think Matt Fisher needs anyone to defend him from me, Sarah," Madigan said, stopping the rocker to turn and look at her. In the shadows under the roof, she was just one more pocket of darkness on the swing.

He got stiffly to his feet and pulled the rocker closer to the glider, then sat down again.

"I wasn't defending him, David, just saying what I think. And I know I'm right. The men around here all think that a gun solves every problem."

"When you've been through a war, then spent the next five or six years worrying that some wild Indians were going to burn you out of house and home, and take your hair for a pony ride while the ashes cooled, I guess you just naturally get to rely on a gun more than some other folks. I mean, my Daddy didn't take a gun down into the mines. There wasn't anything there to shoot but rats, and the noise would have made everybody in the shaft deaf for life anyhow, so he never learned to depend on one. But that doesn't mean that I shouldn't. Not that that's what I'm thinking about, because I'm not."

"You're not like the others, David. You don't reach for a pistol every time somebody disagrees with you."

"No, I guess I don't, but I carried a rifle at Gettysburg and Chickamauga. I'm comfortable with that. And when something happens like happened this morning, I'm willing to pull the trigger."

"That's different." She patted the cushion on the seat of the swing. "Come over here. I can't see you in the dark. Or are you too sore?"

"I was hoping you'd get around to asking me. I thought maybe you were mad at me, or something."

"Not mad, no."

"What, then?"

"Worried, I guess. Worried about what happened this morning, and worried that you might let your temper get the best of you."

"I can't afford to worry about that now, Sassy. I got to get fifty head of saddle stock over to Fort Peterson in a few days, or else. Right now, that's about all I can afford to worry about."

He got to his feet and stretched his legs. Sarah heard the crack of one knee joint, and started to laugh.

"What's so damned funny?"

"My grandfather used to do that with his legs. It sounded like snapping twigs whenever he got up from the dinner table."

Lowering himself gingerly to the glider seat, Madigan leaned toward her menacingly. "You saying I'm getting old, Sarah?"

"Not exactly. But if you think maybe that's what's happening, then maybe I ought to reconsider. Maybe it is."

He pinched her cheek, and she closed the offending hand in both of her own. He spread the fingers and rested the palm against the coolness of her cheek. Feeling the pat of her hands on the back of his own, he said, "Look, I know you're a little worried, but I don't think there's any need. It's never happened before, and unless there's a lot more to it than meets the eye, it likely won't happen again."

"Is that what Matt Fisher thinks?"

"I don't know what, or if, Matt Fisher thinks about it. I just know what I know, and half the time I'm not even sure of that."

She moved closer to him, and let her head rest on his shoulder. He wriggled a bit to make room for her, and circled her waist with his right arm. She let her hand rest on his forearm, the fingers gently stroking the thick bandage under the shirt sleeve. "How's it feel?" she asked.

"It hurts."

"You should have seen Doctor Clemmons, like I told you," she scolded.

Madigan laughed. "By the time I was done with Matt Fisher and Dan Flannery, all I wanted to do was come back home and go to sleep."

"I don't care for that man," Sarah said.

"Who?"

"Dan Flannery. He drinks too much. And I don't like the way he treats Sally."

"Seems to me like he doesn't treat her any way at all. More like he ignores her, is how it seems to me."

"That's exactly what I mean. There's something about him that makes me uneasy. Sometimes when I look at him, my skin crawls. Those eyes of his, so close together, and they never seem to blink. Like a snake's eyes, they are. Cold. It's like looking into a well without a bottom, like you can see all the way inside him, only there's nothing there."

"Sounds to me like you're maybe being a little hard on the man. Sure, he drinks. And I guess he's not the best husband. But he doesn't bother anybody."

"He bothers me."

"You know what I mean. What he does at home is not our business. As long as he doesn't cause anybody any trouble."

Anxious to change the subject, Sarah pecked him on the cheek. "Let me get you a cup of coffee . . . "

"I wouldn't half mind that," Madigan said. "No sugar, just stir it with your little finger. That'll sweeten it up just enough."

"Aren't you the gallant one," she said, tugging on an earlobe with her teeth, nipping until he said, "Ouch! Dammit, Sassy, cut that out!"

She got off the swing before he could retaliate, and he leaned back and let the glider lull him. He closed his eyes again, heard the screendoor hinges squeal once more, then Sarah beginning to hum. He was close to drifting off to sleep, and hoped that Sarah wouldn't be mad if he did.

He heard the loud report, startled and not sure what it was. But he heard breaking glass, he was sure of that, and at the same instant Sarah screamed. Madigan bolted up off the swing, forgetting his aching joints and losing his balance. He landed heavily, and crawled toward the door.

"Sarah!" he called. "Sarah . . . ?"

She didn't answer, and as he tugged the screen door open, another crack sounded behind him, and he heard the thud of a bullet slamming into the door frame, just above his outstretched fingers.

He fell inside, the door banging closed behind him.

Sarah was on the floor, her hands over her ears. She screamed again, and he crawled to her. When his fingers closed over her shoulder, she screamed once more, and he pulled her close to him. "Sarah, honey, are you all right? Sarah? Were you hit?"

She shook her head in the negative, and he looked toward the mantelpiece, knowing that he had to put the lamp out.

Lowering her to the floor again, he whispered. "Wait here. I'll be right back." He rolled across the floor, banging his knee on the hearthstone, then hauled himself to his feet just far enough to grab the lamp. He twisted the wick down, and the cabin was plunged into darkness.

Straightening up, he groped over the mantel until he found his Winchester, and lifted it from the rack.

"David? Where are you?" Sarah whispered.

"Right here, honey. I'm right here . . . "

"What's happening?" she asked. Her voice broke, and she started to sob as he knelt beside her, bracing the rifle against his shoulder and reaching for her in the dark.

"I don't know, Sass. But I'm going to find out." He moved toward the table, where he knew his gunbelt hung on the back of a chair. It swayed away from his grasp then thumped against his fingertips, and he grabbed the holster to hold it still, pulled the Colt out, and lifted the belt from the chair.

"I want you to go into the bedroom and stay there, no matter what happens," he whispered. "Understand? You just stay there and wait for me."

"Yes," she whimpered. And he squeezed her shoulder to reassure her.

"Take this, and don't worry." He held the gun out, felt her hand groping along his arm until her fingers closed over the cylinder. Once she had the gun securely in her grasp, he handed her the gunbelt. "No matter what you hear, don't come out until I come back."

He listened while she crawled across the floor, and when the sound of her knees faded away, he moved toward the front door. He lay on the floor staring out into the darkness, but it was impossible to see anything.

He eased the door open, hoping that whoever was out there wouldn't hear the squeaky hinges. But another shot cracked, and once more the bullet slammed into the front of the cabin. But this time, he'd seen the muzzle flash.

Out on the porch, he let himself off one end, and stepped onto the grass, using the rifle as a crutch to ease his descent.

As near as he could tell, the rifleman was in a clump of pines on top of the hill across from the front of the cabin. He trained his eyes on the crowns of the trees, barely visible against the sky, then moved away from the cabin. Rather than go right up the front of the hill, he wanted to give himself a little edge by working his way around the hill and coming in from behind.

He knew his land pretty well, but it was pitch black, and he had to move slowly to avoid giving himself away. He kept waiting for another gunshot, felt the muscles in his back and shoulders tightening like a cinch. But after waiting for what seemed like an eternity, he could wait no longer. And the gunshot never came.

He started up the hill and had gone no more than twenty feet, when he heard the nicker of a horse, then hoofbeats on the carpet of needles under the pines. He ran then, his aching legs fighting him every step of the way. But he knew that he was too late. Whoever it was had already gone.

5

Madigan stood on the front porch, looking at the bullet holes in the front of the cabin. Shaking his head, as if trying to dislodge some stray fact that might explain what was happening, he backed away, turned, and walked off the porch. Heading straight up the hill to the stand of pines on its crest, he hummed under his breath, trying to get a grip on his emotions. He was used to quick, explosive outbursts of feeling that quickly purged him. This slow boil, rage and uncertainty seething in his gut like some witches' brew, was something new.

When he reached the top of the hill, it didn't take him long to find the scuffs in the needle carpet where the rifleman had lain the night before.

He found three spent shells, too, .44 caliber Winchesters, that told him absolutely nothing. The gun was so common that probably half the men he knew owned one. But he pocketed them anyway, then stood looking down at the house.

It wasn't that long a shot, and he found himself wondering whether the gunman had missed on purpose, perhaps trying to frighten him, rather than kill him. But then he thought about the first shot, the bullet that had smashed through the window, that had narrowly missed Sarah, and he wasn't so sure. He could see the broken window, the jagged shards of glass like glittering spikes around the hole, catching the sun, and shining with brilliant white light. And he got mad all over again.

Kicking the needles, he stomped down the hill to the house. Matt Fisher would be up in the hills in half an hour or so, and he wanted to be there, not just to tell him about the shooting, but to yell and scream. Fisher, whether he liked it or not, whether he deserved it or not, was not just a sheriff now, he was a lightning rod, and Dave Madigan was a thunderbolt right out of Jupiter's quiver, and waiting to explode.

Back on the porch, he called good-bye to Sarah, then walked to the corral, where his horse was already saddled. He had a pack horse ready, too, needing something to carry the extra saddle and the rest of his gear back at the end of the day. He grabbed the hackamore rope of the pack horse, then climbed into the saddle. He clucked to the sorrel and clopped across the yard and into the tall grass leading up and away toward the distant ridge where, not twenty-four hours before, someone had tried to kill him.

On the long ride, he wondered whether he knew the would-be killer. And he wondered, too, whether there might be some reason, other than simple thievery, behind the shooting. But as much as he wracked his brain, he could not come up with an explanation that made any sense.

It was a beautiful morning. The sky was a deep blue, broken only by an occasional cloud so white it hurt the eyes to look at it. The grass, washed clean by the torrential rains, seemed to glow in the sunlight. He had to wade across a creek swollen by the runoff, and the water, normally only eighteen inches deep, came up to his stirrups, and he raised his legs to keep his boots dry, letting the saddle take his full weight for a change.

He spotted a small herd of broncs, and made a mental note to drive them in as soon as he was finished with the sheriff. By the time he reached the ridge where the shooting had happened, he saw a horseman heading along it from the west, and assumed the rider was Matt Fisher. He found his gear, still covered by the slicker, and dismounted, figuring to use the wait to get the gear on the spare horse. He hobbled the sorrel and removed the saddle, transferring it to the spare mount, and jerked the slicker free to uncover his saddle. It was damp, but looked none the worse for wear, and he hoisted it up and dropped it onto the back of the sorrel.

He was finished with the saddle swap as Fisher rode up, just tightening the cinch on the back-up saddle.

"Morning, Dave," Fisher said.

"Matt. Morning."

"I guess we ought to . . ."

Madigan held up a hand. The rage was starting to boil up again, and he interrupted. "Somebody shot up my house last night, Matt."

Fisher was stunned. "What?"

"You heard me. Nearly killed Sarah. Shot through the window, then plunked a couple of slugs into the front of the house, trying to nail me."

"Jesus H. Christ! What in the hell is going on around here? Sarah all right?"

Madigan nodded.

"Thank God for that," Fisher said. Then, looking hard at Madigan, he asked, "You made any enemies I don't know about, Dave?"

Madigan glared at him. "What are you trying to say, Sheriff? Are you trying to say this is *my* fault? Because if you are . . ."

"Hell, no, I'm not saying that. Only it looks to me like there's something going on that don't have nothing to do with stealin' horses, Dave. Or at least, not *just* that, anyhow. Seems to me, a man runs off your horses, he thanks his stars and gets the hell away as soon and as far as he can. If it was me, the last goddamned thing I'd do is come back and try to rub your nose in it. It just don't make no sense, is all."

"Sense or not, it's happening." Madigan stuck

his hand into his pocket. Fishing out the shells, he held them in his palm, extending them to Fisher. "Here," he said, "I picked them up on the hill out front of the house. That's where the shooter was."

"I don't suppose you got a look at him. Or did you?"

Madigan shook his head. "No, I didn't get a look at him. Not even as good as yesterday, and that was no look at all."

"You think it was the same man?"

Madigan sighed in exasperation. "Now how the hell am I supposed to answer that, dammit? I figure it was. Fact is, I *hope* it was. Because I'd rather have one crazy man steal my horses and shoot up my house than think there's two of 'em out there. Because if there's two, God knows how many more there are."

Fisher tilted his head back and scraped his callused fingers against a two-day growth of whiskers under his chin. "I guess we best see if we can find anything. You got work to do, I know that, so I don't want to take up any more of your time than I got to. Why don't you show me where the shooting took place yesterday. Maybe we can find something we can use."

Madigan unhobbled the sorrel and climbed into the saddle. "Follow me," he said. He turned the horse and started along the ridge.

Fisher moved his own horse in alongside Madigan's, and they rode fifty yards or so in silence. Both men kept their eyes on the ground.

The grass was thick, but shorter than on the slope to their right, and in an occasional bare spot, they could see hoofprints, all of them unshod, which meant they were from the dozen stolen horses.

Madigan kept watching the trees to the left, trying to use them as a guide to the location. Finally, after one final glance at a stand of lodgepoles, he reined in. "Just about here was where he stopped and cut loose."

He swung down from the saddle, and let the sorrel walk off a way. When the sheriff dismounted, they walked along the ridge a few yards, stopping every couple of steps. "Just hoofprints, is all I see, Dave," Fisher said.

Madigan nodded. "Me, too. But I . . . "

"Hold on," Fisher blurted, bending to one knee and leaning over to look at a muddy spot no bigger than a saucer. "Lookee here!"

Madigan stooped down to see.

"Shoe got a chunk missing, see here?" The sheriff pointed with an extended finger. "Looks almost like a capital letter D, don't it, the way the outside edge runs straight along the rim of the shoe?"

"Got to be the rustler, because my stock was unshod."

"Let's look a little more, see if we can find anything else. He was using a rifle, you said, right?"

"Yep. Fired four or five times, maybe more. It all happened so fast, I'm not really sure. He cut loose further back, then when he stopped, he fired a bunch of times." He was in a squat now, creeping along, sifting the grass with his fingers. Matt Fisher was on hands and knees, also raking through the shiny blades.

"Lookit this, Dave," Fisher said. He held up a spent shell. Like the ones from the top of hill back at the cabin, it was a .44 Winchester. They combed through the grass more intently now, and between them found four more cartridge cases, each identical to the others.

"I reckon there's no doubt it was the same shooter, Dave," Fisher concluded.

"Maybe. Same ammunition, anyhow. But it's not iron clad."

"It will be, you find a print with that D notch in it back at the house."

"I'll check when I get home," Madigan said.

"Look, I know you got work to do. There ain't nothing more you can do on this up here anyhow, so why don't you get to it. I'm gonna follow these tracks a while, see if they lead anyplace interesting. With that rain yesterday, the ground was plenty soft. As long as the prints weren't washed away, maybe I can crawl right up that rustler's backbone and tap him on the shoulder."

Madigan knew Fisher was right, but part of him wanted to go along for the ride. Fisher seemed to know what he was thinking, and clapped him on the shoulder. "Look, Dave, if I find him, I'll let you know first thing. But I'm gonna bring him in, I ain't gonna shoot him. I know you'd just as soon put a bullet through his head, but that won't do nothing but get you in a whole lot of hot water. You got Sarah to think about, and you got that contract to fill, too. So . . . "

"You'll let me know?"

Fisher smiled, then patted his pocket for his tobacco pouch. "Course I will." He jerked the pouch free, opened it, and rolled a cigarette. Striking a match on his gun belt, he lit the cigarette, took a puff, then exhaled the smoke in a thin stream that rippled on the breeze before breaking apart. "You know, don't you, that it's gonna be hard to convict this sonofabitch, even if I find him."

"Why?"

"Because you didn't see him clear enough to identify him, at least that's what you think, anyhow. Not yesterday, and not last night. The .44 shells don't mean much, neither, since you could throw a rock into a crowd and be pretty sure you'll hit somebody who uses them. That chip in the shoe gives us a little hook, but it ain't enough to hang him on."

"So what's the point of going after him at all?"

"If I can figure out who it is, I'll bring him in. Maybe you saw more than you think you did. But even if you didn't, maybe it'll put some pressure on him. Then we can watch him close. He'll make a mistake sooner or later, and when he does, we'll be ready for him. But we can't tip our hand. Fact is, if I do run him down, I might not even bring him in, unless I got more reason than I got now. I find your stock in his corral, for example, then it's a done deal. Or if I find some of Dan Flannery's cows in his barn. But you and I both know that ain't too likely. So maybe what we got to do is hold our water. We lay out a few snares, then we wait for him to ride into one of 'em. We'll have to see what we see."

"That sounds nice, Matt, but it doesn't get my horses back."

"I know, I know, but you got to be patient. Half the business of the law is sitting on your hands with your eyes half shut, keepin' secrets to yourself. Speaking of which, don't say nothing about the chipped shoe, not even to Sarah. As long as just you and me know about it, maybe it'll give us the opening we need."

Madigan took a deep breath. "It really burns my ass to pretend nothing happened. You know that, don't you Matt?"

"I know it, yeah. I do. But I also know it's the best chance we got to nail this thieving bastard. And that's what really counts, ain't it?"

"I guess so, yeah. I guess so."

Fisher clapped him on the shoulder again. "'Course it is," he said. He tucked the shells into his pocket and headed back toward his horse. Madigan stayed there, watching him, feeling the boiling in his gut. Even knowing that Fisher was right didn't make him feel any better.

The sheriff swung into the saddle. "Go on, Dave, get them horses together. That's what you got to concentrate on."

He waved and clapped his knees against the horse's ribs, clucking to him and moving along the ridge, his eyes locked on the ground. Madigan watched him for a hundred yards or so, then sighed and walked to his horse.

6

It had been a long day. Madigan had found two small herds of horses, one of eleven, and one of seven. The eighteen head were just the beginning. He still needed almost twice that many to make his obligation, but he kept telling himself that he had to start somewhere, and that if he waited until he found a herd of fifty or more, it was possible that hell would freeze over that same day.

He'd fashioned a makeshift corral out of rope, and penned the seven in. The larger group was led by a big roan stallion, and he'd had a hell of a time getting a rope on him. He'd tried driving the animals, but the roan was too cagey, and he kept leading them off at a gallop as soon as Madigan tried to push them toward the holding pen. It would have been a whole lot easier if he had help, but there wasn't room for that in the budget, so he sucked it up and chased the big roan for two miles before getting a rope to settle over his proud head.

The stallion resisted the rope, rearing up and slashing at the sky with his hooves, but Madigan held his ground, and once the roan realized that the man on the other end of the rope had as much determination as he did, he settled down. All during the contest, the other ten horses had stood off to one side, uncertain whether to light out on their own or wait to see what happened.

But when Madigan started down hill toward the pen, they all fell in behind the roan, faithful to him even in his defeat. Men should be as loyal, Madigan thought. When he reached the pen, he knew the pinto that had been running at the head of the smaller herd might give him trouble, so he dismounted, tied off the roan, and circled the holding pen with a lariat, looking for a chance to rope the pinto. He'd lead them both on a rope, and if God was willing, the other sixteen head would follow along.

Once the pinto was roped and docile again, Madigan looped the two leads to his saddle horn, and headed home. It was five miles, and the ropes sawed at his left leg the whole time, but he didn't want to try to hold the leads in his hand, just in case the stallions decided to try him out one more time. When he reached the last hill overlooking his cabin, he slowed a bit, watching the house. He could still see the broken glass, the sharp edges of the shattered pane orange in the late afternoon light.

He'd left the larger of the two corrals open, and cantered right on through the gate, the roan getting antsy now, the pinto sensing it and tugging on his rope a little. But by then, it didn't matter, they were inside the fence, and he dismounted, tying both leads to a fence rail and sprinting back to the gate to shoo the last couple of stragglers inside. He closed the gate then and walked back to get his mount and pack horse, leading them to the gate, opening it, and tugging them on through.

He saw Sarah on the porch and waved. She dried her hands on her apron before waving back, and while he unsaddled the pack horse, she crossed the yard to stand with him.

"Looks like you made a good start, David," she said.

"A start, yeah. But I still got a long way to go. I wish to Christ we had enough money to fence those meadows, then I wouldn't have to ride all over creation looking for something that's already mine."

"Maybe next spring, we can . . ."

Madigan laughed. "You know how many times we've said that? You know how many springs have come and gone without one damn post being sunk?"

She sighed. "Yes, I guess you're right. Still, with a little luck we might . . ."

"With a little luck, we might not lose the ranch. It'll take a whole lot more than a little to get that damn fence built."

Sarah didn't answer right away, and he sensed that something was on her mind. He turned the pack horse loose in the smaller corral before turning to look at her.

"What's wrong, Sassy?"

She hunched her shoulders and lowered her chin, as if trying to ward off a blow from an unseen hand. "Nothing, I guess. Matt Fisher was here this afternoon."

Madigan raised an inquiring eyebrow. "Oh, really? What'd he want? I just saw him this morning."

"I know. He told me. He . . . well, he's arrested someone for stealing the horses."

"I didn't expect that. Not from the way he was talking this morning."

"He said you'd be surprised. He wants you to come to town, see if you recognize the man he's holding."

"Anyone we know?"

Sarah shook her head. "I don't think so. He said it was somebody from over near Sullivan. A Mexican settler, he said. A farmer."

"Well, I suppose I better go on into town and see what's what."

"You want dinner first? You must be hungry."

Madigan bent to pick up the spare saddle, shouldered it with a grunt, and said, "Sassy, if I sit down now, I won't get up for a week. I'd better just get on in and see about this. Matt say how long he was going to be in his office?"

"He said he'd wait for you. He seemed pretty sure you'd want to come in right away."

"Then I guess it's only right I do. I don't want to keep him waiting there all evening. Millie'll skin him alive, unless he blames it on me, in which case it'll be my hide she peels with that sharp tongue of hers."

"Don't be long, David, all right? I'll keep dinner for you."

"Don't bother, hon. I'll get something to eat in town."

"You sure? It's no trouble."

"I'm sure."

He hugged her, trying not to give in to the temptation to stay home with her. It was beginning to feel like he never saw her anymore. And all afternoon, he had worried about her. What would happen to him if he lost her, he wondered. He squeezed her hard, then forced himself to pull away. He climbed back onto the sorrel and nudged the horse close to her. She let one hand rest on his thigh, and he leaned over to run his fingers through her auburn curls. "I'll be home as soon as I can, Sass."

"I'll wait up." She backed away, her hands clenched, fingers interlaced, suspended just below her chin. It looked almost as if she were praying.

Before heading for town, he wanted to check the top of the hill, where the shooter had lain, and he nudged the sorrel straight for the clump of pines. Dismounting at the crest of the hill, he let the sorrel walk behind him. He'd have to move past the trees to find anything, because the thick layer of brittle needles wouldn't show him anything. But he could follow the scuff marks on the carpet, and when he reached the open ground beyond the trees, he slowed up, bending over and looking at the grass.

He found a few hoofprints, but none of them was complete, and none clear enough to show him what he was hoping to see. But as he moved downhill, he found a couple of muddy places, now baked hard by the day's sun, and three hoofprints. One place, deep in the mud and at the end of a wide groove where the hoof had slipped a little, he found a whole print.

He knelt down and leaned over it, shielding his eyes from the sun to see it more clearly. And there it was, the same D-shaped notch out of the shoe. He stared at it for several seconds, almost as if he expected it to tell him something. Then, getting back to his feet, he climbed onto the sorrel and kicked it hard enough to startle it, and headed for Clarion.

Town was bustling, and nearly every hitching post had at least one horse. Several wagons lined the streets, hard up against the boardwalks. He wondered whether something had happened. The saloons, and there were quite a few, were crowded, and as he headed for the sheriff's office, he could hear the raucous laughter that seemed to pour out of the same bottles as the whiskey. A loud piano, slightly out of tune, was being thumped by someone who had at best a rudimentary knowledge of music. But judging by the rumble of conversation spilling out of the saloon, no one inside cared very much.

He dismounted in front of the sheriff's office, and Matt Fisher appeared in the doorway as Madigan hitched the sorrel.

"You got my message, I see," Fisher said.

Madigan climbed onto the boardwalk. "Sarah said you arrested someone, is that right?"

Fisher nodded. "Sure is."

"From what you were saying this morning, I thought you were maybe going to wait a while, even if you found somebody."

"Didn't have to wait, Dave. Got him dead to rights. Come on in and have a peek at your man."

Fisher turned to step inside, and Madigan followed him. The sheriff reached for a key ring hanging from a peg on the wall behind his desk, clutched the heavy keys in his fist, and rattled them as he walked to the door leading to the cell-block.

"Take a look, 'fore I open the door." Fisher stepped aside and Madigan moved close to the heavy metal door. Leaning against the bars mounted high in the center, he peered into the gloomy interior of the back room. Blocks of orange light, barred with shadow, lay on the floor. Madigan saw dust motes swirling in the brilliance and, in the shadows beyond them, a man sitting on a bunk, his head bent, his head sagging toward his lap. Madigan couldn't see the man's face, and he looked at Fisher, stepping back for the sheriff to open the door.

The key ground in the lock, and the heavy door swung open without a sound, until it banged into the wall behind it, a single, dull thud. Fisher led the way into the cell-block and walked past the only occupied cell.

Madigan stopped in front of it, and looked at the man, who still stared at his lap. His hands were restless, but he seemed uninterested in who the visitor might be.

"Hey, Señor," Fisher said. "You got company."

The man raised his head slowly, and looked at Fisher, then at Madigan. He took a deep breath, puffed out his cheeks, then expelled the air in a single rush. He was small and dark. A heavy, black mustache drooped forlornly, framing a soft mouth that pursed and unpursed its lips with nervous regularity.

"What do you think, Dave?"

Madigan didn't answer.

"That look like him, or not? I know you didn't get a real good look at him, but . . . that's him, isn't it? I mean, it's got to be."

"I don't know, Matt. It was dark, it was raining like hell, and he was nearly a hundred yards away at the closest."

"Could be him, though, don't you think?"

Madigan wiped his palms on his jeans, then moved closer and curled his hands around the bars. The man had lost interest, and was looking at his lap again, as if the visitors had already left him alone.

"I don't think it's him, Matt, to tell the truth."

"Sure it is. It has to be."

"Why's that?"

"I followed them tracks. They went right to his house. There was two of Flannery's cows up behind the house, running with his stock, not that he had a whole lot."

"Did you ask him about the cows?"

"'Course I did."

"What'd he say?"

"Says he bought them. He says he's got a bill of sale, but he didn't show it to me. Says he couldn't find it when he went to look for it."

"You check his horse?"

"Yeah."

"And?"

Fisher shook his head. "Nothing. But he could have changed the shoes."

"Did they look new?"

Fisher patted his stomach, then shook his head, "No, they didn't, actually. And that bothers me a bit, to tell you the truth. Still. The tracks, the stolen cows, the . . . "

"They were not stolen, Señor! I pay for them. I told you that." The prisoner was on his feet now, hands gripping the bars so tightly that the bronze skin on the back of his hands was almost white at the knuckles.

"You stole them, all right, amigo. You know it

and I know it. Come on, Dave, I'll buy you a drink."

He moved toward his office, leaving Madigan alone for a moment. Madigan looked at the man closely. Now that he was on his feet, it was obvious that he was on the small side, maybe too small to be the horse thief, but he wasn't sure.

Madigan backed toward the door, the prisoner's eyes locked on his, not pleading, not belligerent, just questioning. And as Madigan backed through the doorway, he found those silent questions echoing in the back of his mind. Even the dull clang of the heavy door closing failed to drown them out.

The sheriff sat down at his desk, and pointed to a chair. "Pull up a seat a minute, Dave. You look like something's on your mind."

Madigan shook his head. "No, I just . . . hell, I don't know what it is."

"Look, I appreciate the fact that you ain't sure about the Mex. Jail ain't a good place to be, and nobody wants to see a man behind bars if he don't belong there. I know I sure as hell don't. And If I wasn't sure about it, that man wouldn't be there right now." He tapped his fingers on the desk, then added, "Pretty sure, anyhow."

"You said you followed the tracks to his home."

"That's right. I did."

"Did you go past, or did you stop when you got there."

"I stopped, why? It seemed pretty clear I'd got to where I was goin'."

Madigan shrugged his shoulders and looked at the door to the cell-block. "I was just thinking that if the horse thief went past his place, maybe . . . I guess that doesn't make any sense." He looked at Fisher, hoping the sheriff understood what he was groping toward, and not even sure what it was.

"Think about it for a minute, Dave. Put yourself in his shoes, or if not his, then those of the rustler. If you was running somebody's stock, would you ride right past a man's house? So close you could smell bacon fryin'?"

"Not if I could help it, no. But it was dark, it was raining hard. Hell, maybe whoever it was didn't know the house was there. Maybe . . . maybe he's not from around here."

"I'd like to believe that, just like you would. Hell, a man don't like to think his neighbors are stealing from him. But look, I got his rifle. It's a Winchester .44, same as the shooter used on you. The shells are Winchesters, too. I got his sidearm, also." He jerked a thumb over his shoulder to where a gunbelt hung on a wooden rack.

Madigan glanced at it, then got to his feet and walked to the front window. "I'm just not sure, is all, Matt," he said, looking out into the street. "I'm just not sure. And I don't like it."

"I appreciate that, Dave. I truly do. But it ain't like it's just your word, you know. I got plenty of reason to hold him. There's them two cows, for starters."

"You know as well as I do, Matt, that beeves wander off all the time. They run into some other cattle, sometimes they fall in with 'em. Maybe that's all it was. If he'd stolen them, wouldn't he have doctored the brands?"

"If he was smart enough, sure. And if he'd had time, which maybe he didn't, because he was too damn busy running off your stock."

"Then where are my horses? If he's stolen them, where are they?" Madigan turned around and walked over to the desk, leaned forward to brace himself with his hands on the front edge, and rocked on his heels. "Where are they?" he repeated.

"Oh, hell, how'm I supposed to know. Maybe he sold them already. Maybe he's got them hid out in the hills. You could hide a thousand horses up there and it would take weeks to find them, unless you knew right where to look."

Once more, Madigan glanced at the gunbelt hanging behind Fisher's desk. Narrowing his eyes, he sucked on a tooth and stared at it.

"Something wrong, Dave?" Fisher asked.

Instead of answering, Madigan moved around the desk and took the gunbelt from the rack. "This is his, you said?"

"That's right."

Madigan wrapped it around his waist, then turned to face the sheriff. "You notice anything, Matt?"

"It's a gunbelt, same as a thousand others. Colt .45 pistol, same as two thousand others. What the hell am I supposed to notice?"

"Look closely."

"I *am* lookin' dammit. But what the hell I am I lookin' *for*."

"The man's left-handed, Matt. The man who stole my horses was right-handed. I remember seeing the holster on his right hip every time the lightning flashed. I close my eyes, and I can see it plain as day."

"You sure about that, Dave?"

"As sure as I'm standing here. You got the wrong man, Matt!"

Fisher leaned back in his chair. "Damn, I knew it was too good to be true." He tilted forward, took the gunbelt from around Madigan's waist, and curled the belt around the holster, then let it drop into his lap. "Goddamn . . . Then how do you explain them tracks?"

"You said you checked his horse and you didn't find the chipped shoe. Maybe it's just like I said. Maybe whoever run off my stock didn't realize where he was. Hell, in that storm you could have ridden within fifty feet of my place and not realized it was there, unless the lightning flashed while you were passing by. Maybe that's all it was."

Fisher shook his head. "Nope, that ain't all it was. That much I am sure of. Them tracks went right down to his corral. A blind man maybe wouldn't have seen it, but anybody else would have, and the blind man most likely would have run smack into the fence. If that wasn't his horse made them tracks, then they were made by somebody he knows. Maybe a partner."

"You can't hold him on something that flimsy, Matt."

"Hell, I know that. I don't like it, but I know it." Fisher got to his feet. "Come on, let's go have that drink. I'll think about it some, make sure I ain't overlooked anything. If I ain't, then I'll cut him loose as soon as I get back."

"Why don't you let him go now, Matt? You know as well as I do that nothing is going to change after a glass of whiskey."

"That's probably true, Dave. But being a lawman ain't as simple as what's right and wrong. There's some things you got to consider that don't have nothing to do with the law."

"Like what?"

"People is what. Folks around here are pretty het up, what with you losing stock, somebody takin' a pot shot at you, Dan Flannery missing some cows. They're a little rambunctious, and I want to get the feel of things before I do something hasty. Or stupid."

"Maybe it was hasty bringing that poor bastard in in the first place."

Fisher rubbed his chin thoughtfully. He didn't look happy, and Madigan didn't blame him. For a few seconds, it seemed as if he weren't going to respond at all. But finally, he cleared his throat, and said, "Well, now, you might be right. But that's water under the bridge. I can't undo it as simple as I'd like. I got to worry about what might happen next. Fact is, that's why I want to wander down to the Arrowhead, kind of get the feel of things, see if I can't tell what folks are thinkin'."

"All right. Let's go, then. The sooner I get home, the sooner I can get to sleep so I can get up before dawn and bust my ass another whole damn day, trying to get those horses ready."

He walked to the door and held it open, hoping his haste would rub off on Fisher. But the sheriff didn't seem to be in much of a hurry. He buckled the gunbelt, hung it from the rack, and checked the door leading to the cell-block. Only when he'd run out of busywork did he head toward the door.

Outside, he looked up the street, then extended an arm. "See all them wagons, and all them horses, Dave? They're all here because the news spread so quick about the Mex. Folks want to know what's happening, so they sit down with a glass of beer in front of them and listen to the truth get bent all out of shape. Once it's twisted beyond all recognition, they tuck it into the back of their minds. They're content, they believe it, and they come home. Seems sometimes like there ain't no news so bad it wouldn't benefit by bein' a little worse. Hell, half the men in town probably think you got killed, not withstanding the fact that some of them seen you with their own eyes just yesterday afternoon."

Madigan laughed. "Sounds like you got a

pretty jaundiced view of human nature, Matt."

"You pin it on with the badge, Dave. I only hope I can take it off as easy as the badge, once it's time. Millie thinks I can't. She says I been ruined forever, and there are times when I think maybe she's about right."

They headed up the street to the Arrowhead Saloon. As they were about to enter, Fisher said, "Now, this was my idea, so I'm buying. Don't give me no argument once we get inside."

Madigan smiled. "You ever know me to turn down a free drink, Matt?"

"I never knew *anybody* turn down a free drink, come to think of it," Fisher laughed.

The sheriff led the way inside, and the bartender, a burly Irishman named Paddy Collins, waved a damp towel in their direction. Cupping his hands to be heard over the din, he yelled, "Come on in, boys. Drinks are on me."

Fisher waved, then leaned close to Madigan to whisper, "Seems like they're in a party mood. That ain't necessarily a good sign."

Every head in the place had turned toward the door, and the conversation dwindled away to a buzz as Madigan and the sheriff pushed through the throng to belly up to the bar. Collins wiped the expanse of bar in front of them, even though it already gleamed, and asked, "What'll you boys be havin'?"

"I'll take a rye, Paddy," Fisher told him.

Collins looked at Madigan then, waiting for his order. "Just a beer, I think, Paddy."

"Oh, now, come on, Davey boy. You got some celebratin' to do, seems like to me. Maybe you ought to have something a little better. After all, it's free." Collins laughed, wiped the bar again, then leaned on his elbows waiting for Madigan to reconsider.

"All right, I'll take a bourbon and water."

"That's better, but not good enough. Madigan, that's Irish. Maybe a little nip of Jameson's is what you need, Davey. I'll get it for you, and if you don't like it, then you can name your poison."

As Collins moved down the bar, chuckling and shaking his head, Madigan turned to look at the crowd. The conversation was slowly returning to its deafening volume. He saw Dan Flannery sitting at a table, looking his way, and talking to someone Madigan didn't recognize.

The thump of a glass on the bar behind him announced the arrival of his drink, and as he started to turn, he saw Flannery get to his feet and start working his way through the throng toward him.

Fisher saw him, too, and whispered, "Here comes trouble, unless I miss my guess. Wait'll he hears I'm gonna turn the Mex loose."

"Don't tell him. He looks like he's already loaded. Better let him hear it tomorrow morning, when he's sober," Madigan suggested.

Flannery squeezed in between them, draped an arm over each man's shoulder, and said, "Nice work, Sheriff. Fact is, I never figured you to get the job done so soon. If ever." He laughed, and squeezed Fisher's shoulder. "But it just goes to show you, don't it?"

"Yeah, don't it," Fisher said.

Turning to Madigan, Flannery leaned forward a bit. He was unsteady on his feet, and his head kept wobbling. His boozy breath swirled in a noxious cloud, and Madigan was starting to wish he'd gone straight home.

"How about that sonofabitch, Dave? How about him?"

"Which sonofabitch is that? Who are you talking about, Dan?"

"Mexican sumbitch tried to blow your head off, he did. Nice to see he's gonna swing for it."

"You're a bit premature on that, aren't you Dan?" Fisher asked. "Hell, the man ain't even been tried. Fact is, there's a long way to go before anybody knows whether he's guilty or not."

Once more the rancher's head wobbled. Flannery had a cock-eyed grin even when sober, and with a few drinks under his belt, he could pass for the village idiot. All he needed was a little drool on his chin, and from the look of him, it wasn't far off. "We know he's guilty. Hell, he had my cows in his herd. What more proof do you need?"

"That's up to the judge and jury, Dan."

Flannery laughed. "Yeah. Well, I'll be the judge *and* the jury. And I think he's guilty as hell. Damn little greaser shootin' at my friend Dave, here. Ought to make short work of the bastard, you ask me."

"Fortunately, Dan," Fisher pointed out, "no one *has* asked you."

"Don't matter. Folks around here know what's what."

8

Madigan was up before the sun. He wanted to throw himself into his work, but there was nothing he could do to round up more horses until it was light enough to see. To kill time, he went to the barn carrying a pair of kerosene lamps, and once inside, lit them both and hung them from hooks on a crossbeam. Grabbing a broom by the handle, tightening both hands around it as if he wanted to throttle the already lifeless wood, he started to sweep out a stall.

The sweet stink of rotting straw and cow dung swirled up around him as he worked and he wanted to gag, but he kept on flailing at the ground, paying less attention to his success than

72

to the energy he expended. He was mad at everybody and everything, precisely because there was no one at all to be mad at. Except the horse thief, and he was convinced the Mexican was not the man.

But whether he was or not, there was still a contract to be filled, and until he had done that, he would have no peace. The mound of matted straw was growing, and he shoved it toward the door of the barn, leaving trails of the stinking stuff behind. When he had the worst of the mound outside, he stopped to lean on the broom for a moment, staring at the house.

The broken window was still there to remind him of what had been going on, only less visible now because he'd covered it over with greased paper. He had the new glass, but he hadn't found the time to replace the broken pane. That would have to wait until evening. He could see it only because Sarah was up now, a lamp lit in the room beyond, and the ugly paper seemed like an insult, a thumbed nose, telling him that everything he owned was going to hell in a handbasket. And reminding him, too, that there was precious little he could do about any of it.

He shoved the mound of damp straw ahead of him with jerks of the broom until Sarah came out onto the porch.

He saw her outlined against the light spilling through the doorway, leaning a little to peer into the darkness. "David?" she called. "Where are you?"

"Right here, hon," he answered.

"Come get breakfast."

"I'm not hungry."

"Well, it's ready, so you might as well come in and eat."

He hadn't lied. He *wasn't* hungry, but he knew he needed to eat something to keep body and soul together. There was no point in making himself weak when he needed every bit of strength he could muster for the coming days.

Leaning the broom against the open door of the barn, he kicked the ground a few times to remove the worst of the glutinous muck clinging to his boots, then scraped them on dry ground a few paces as he dragged toward the porch. Once up the steps, he used a brush mounted near the door to finish cleaning the boots, then went inside.

The table was already set. Sarah was pouring coffee. "You never told me what happened yesterday," she said, walking back to the stove with the coffee pot and grabbing a heavy mitten before picking up a frying pan. Back at the table she spooned scrambled eggs and fried potatoes onto his plate, gave herself a smaller portion, then set the pan down on a trivet before taking a seat.

"Matt Fisher had somebody in jail all right, but it wasn't the right man, so he was going to let him go."

Sarah looked at him curiously. "You're sure it was the wrong man?"

"Sure as I can be. It was some Mexican man

named Rivera, a settler, has a place a few miles east of here. But it wasn't him."

"Why did Sheriff Fisher arrest him in the first place?"

Madigan shrugged. "I don't know. I think he was so anxious to wrap things up, he let his enthusiasm get the best of him. But after we talked, he decided I was right."

"How terrible for that poor man!"

"I don't know if I'd go that far. Hell, nothing happened to him."

"But you know how people are. Somebody gets thrown in jail, a lot of people think he's guilty of something, never mind what. After all, they think, he wouldn't have been arrested at all, if he hadn't done *something*."

"Maybe so," Madigan said, sipping his coffee, "but I got enough troubles of my own without worrying about somebody else's problems."

"What is Sheriff Fisher going to do now?"

"Keep looking, I guess." Madigan forked some potatoes into his mouth and looked at Sarah while he chewed. When he'd swallowed, he added, "Not that I expect that to amount to much. Matt did his best, but it was just about impossible to find the man. The thing that scares me is that whoever it was came looking for me, and for the life of me, I can't figure out why he did it."

"Maybe it's not just about the stolen horses, David. Maybe it's about something else."

Madigan let his fork drop to his plate with a

clatter. "What the hell are you talking about, Sass? What else could it be about?"

"Maybe you'll know the answer to that if Sheriff Fisher finds out who it was." She sipped her own coffee, as if there was no way around her logic, smiling sweetly at him over the rim of her cup.

Madigan was anxious to change the subject. "I figure I can get another fifteen or twenty head down today. If I'm right, I'll be able to get the rest tomorrow. Then it'll take me two days to get to Fort Peterson. If I'm lucky."

"Is there anything I can do to help?"

Madigan shook his head. "Nope. I'll manage."

"If you change your mind, let me know. Don't be too proud to ask. I know how you are."

Scooping up the last of his breakfast, Madigan paused with the fork suspended just below his open mouth. "Oh, and how is that?" he asked.

"Stubborn as a mule and proud as a peacock. A particularly difficult combination for a woman to cope with."

"You've coped fine the last few years, near as I can tell."

She gave him another exaggerated smile. "And don't think it's been easy, mister."

"If I weren't so damned busy, I'd give you what for . . . "

"I'm no fool. I pick my spots," she said, laughing, then sticking out her tongue.

Madigan pushed back his chair and got up. "I'll be up north, Sassy, if anybody's looking for me. Not that I expect anybody, but these days you never know . . . "

He walked outside into the morning light still tinged with red. At the barn, he picked up his tack, lugged it to the corral, and saddled the sorrel for what seemed like the thousandth time in the last hour. He would have liked nothing better than to grab a fishing pole and spend an afternoon lolling half asleep in the grass, drowning a few worms, and watching the clouds change shape. But that just wasn't in the cards.

He tried not to look at the house as it dwindled away behind him, knowing that Sarah was there alone, and that if he was right and the Mexican was not the man who'd tried to kill him, then someone else had, and whoever that someone else might be was still out there somewhere.

By quarter to eight, he was up in the hills, sitting on a ridge, looking once more through the glasses, trying to find his stock. He wished that he had been better organized, had more warning of the contract, because he'd have gathered the animals a hell of a lot sooner. But that was the way his life had been lately. At times, he felt like a blindfolded man tiptoeing from boulder to boulder across a river at flood. One mistake, one false step, even a hesitation, and everything, him included, just might be swept away.

Using the glasses, he searched the valley below him, looking for a reasonably sized herd. But instead of his own horses, he caught a glimpse of a solitary man on horseback, dogging him, coming upcountry the same way he had. At the moment, the man was heading into the bottom end of a rocky draw more than a mile away, too far for Madigan to recognize him, even through the binoculars.

But recognize him or not, there was no way he wasn't going to get a greeting. Madigan headed into a stand of trees, letting the sorrel walk, then, as soon as he was out of sight from the draw far below him, he kicked hell out of the horse and pushed it as hard as he could. A mile west, where the ridge started to drop away, he angled downhill at a dead gallop, and kept the sorrel running flat out for half a mile.

Reining in, he dismounted in a hurry, grabbing the Winchester as his a feet hit the ground. This time, by God, wasn't nobody gonna sneak up on him or find him otherwise unprepared. He tied the horse in a clump of scrubby pines, little dead trees that grew in a ring surrounded by the towering lodgepoles. Sprinting then, he worked his way through brush and boulders, heading toward the mouth of the draw. He couldn't stop to see whether the rider had made it yet, but didn't think he had. The man, apparently confident that Madigan did not know he was there, had been taking it easy. That was his mistake.

Madigan found cover in a cluster of boulders about fifty yards north of the opening into the draw. He hunkered down among the rocks, working the Winchester lever as quietly as he could to chamber a round, then wiggled around until he was halfway comfortable. He could see the entire mouth of the draw, and a good thirty or forty yards down into it, despite its zigzag path.

He listened for the sound of approaching hooves, but heard nothing at first. He was tempted to get up and move closer, but worried that he might get caught in the open. Whoever it was might just be an innocent traveller, or maybe even someone looking for him, but if it was the shooter, he didn't want to make his job any easier, so Madigan stayed where he was, his eyes pined to the draw mouth. He was afraid even to blink, and cursed in annoyance every time his straining lids broke his line of sight.

When he heard the echoing nicker of a horse some way down the draw, he relaxed a bit, confident now that he had the upper hand. He relaxed his fingers in the trigger guard, and listened to see if he could hear anything that might tell him whether the rider was still alone. It hadn't even dawned on him until that moment that he had been assuming one man when it might just as easily be five or ten.

But the hooves sounded lonely, and he was pretty sure it was only one horse. He could hear the click of horseshoes on the broken rock littering the floor of the draw, and sometimes the clatter of stones kicked loose or skidding under the horse's weight.

As the sound came closer, he could feel the

hair rising on the back of his neck, something he hadn't felt since the war, and it made him tremble for a moment. Steeling himself, whispering under his breath to get a grip on his nerves, he chewed his lower lip and moved the lead sight of the Winchester back and forth in a silent sweep from edge to edge of the draw. He still saw nothing, but the sound of hooves was coming closer.

He saw a puff of smoke, then the brim of a hat as the rider came into view. He let his finger rest on the trigger, just to be sure. And cursed, when he recognized Dan Flannery.

For a split second, it crossed his mind that maybe Flannery was the shooter, but the thought made him feel just a little bit foolish and, pulling off the target, he lowered the hammer on the Winchester.

Shaking his head in annoyance, Madigan straightened, then stepped out of the rocks. His sudden appearance startled Flannery's horse, and the big gray reared up, nearly throwing the woolgathering rider from the saddle.

"Jesus Christ, Davey!" Flannery exploded "You scared the vinegar right out of the jar. What in the hell are you doing there?"

"I saw somebody coming, and I didn't know who it was, so . . . ." He let Flannery fill in the rest of the explanation. "What are you doing up here?"

"Looking for you. Sarah said you were up here running some horses down, and I figured I might as well come on up."

"I don't have time for chewing the fat, Dan," Madigan told him.

"I ain't here to chew the fat. I wanted to talk to you about Rivera, that Mex Matty Fisher had locked up. Until you put a bug in his ear, that is."

"What about him?"

"How come you said he wasn't the one tried to gun you?"

"Because he wasn't the man."

"You don't know that."

"Sure I do. I wouldn't have said anything, otherwise."

"A lot of people ain't too happy with you, right now, Davey."

"That right? Why?'

"They don't like it that you'd take up for a greaser. Especially one with the habit of stealing horses and shooting at neighbors."

"He wasn't the man, Dan. I'm sure of it."

"How can you be so sure? He's a greaser. He had my beeves, and that was enough for Matt Fisher. Should be enough for you, too, the way folks see it."

"By folks, do you mean to include yourself, Dan?" Madigan asked. He was getting impatient, and Flannery's meddlesome ways were not calculated to soothe his frazzled nerves. "Or are you just talking about other folks?"

"Course I include myself. The man took my cattle. He took your horses. I figure we both got an interest in seein' him locked up. Until they can hoist him a little."

"Well, you're wrong, Dan. What I have an interest in is seeing the man who tried to kill me put behind bars. I don't think just anyone will do, just because it happens to be easy."

"That's not what it's all about, Madigan. It's about seein' to it that nobody run off stock that don't belong to him. That greaser ain't no different than anybody else. Those are the rules, and he's got to live by 'em, same as me and you."

"Far as I know, he does. Far as you know, too. Unless you know more than me and Matt Fisher."

"I was talking to some men in town. They figure they might have to do Matt's job for him. I figured you'd go along, until Fisher told me it was your idea to cut the greaser loose. Which I plain do not understand."

"Look, Dan, somebody shot up my house. Nearly killed my wife. Now, if I thought Rivera was the man, don't you think I'd say so? What reason would I have to want to see him loose?"

Flannery smiled. "Well, it occurred to me that maybe you don't have no more faith in Matty Fisher than the rest of us. Maybe you figured you could handle it your own self, get it done sooner and cleaner."

Madigan took a deep breath. It was all he could do to keep from tearing Flannery off his horse and kicking him back down the draw. But instead, he clenched his fists and said, "That ain't the way I do things, Dan. Now, if you'll excuse me, I have work to do."

Flannery seemed unruffled. "Sure, I understand. But if something happens to the greaser, I know you wouldn't mind. I'll just tell . . . "

"You'll tell nobody nothing, dammit. Now git on out of here before I lose my temper."

Flannery gave him a gap-toothed grin, touched the brim of his hat, and said, "*Adios, ah-mee-go.*"

9

Madigan was finishing his second run of the day. It was late afternoon and he was forcing himself to keep his eyes open. But at least he had all the horses he needed. All he had to worry about now was driving them a hundred miles without losing any of them. And hoping they met with the approval of the finicky Major Harrison Fletcher. He was planning on leaving first thing in the morning and, with a little luck, he'd make it to Fort Peterson a day early, not that it would improve the price. But every day early was a day sooner he could expect to get paid, or so he told himself. The fact was that he was sort of looking forward to rubbing Fletcher's nose in it a little.

By the time he was heading down into the valley, he wondered whether or not he'd fall out of the saddle before he reached the corral. One thing kept him going. He'd put Dan Flannery's advice on to simmer and the fire was still burning. The man had colossal nerve, telling him that he ought to insist that Rivera be kept in jail. And he wondered, too, whether Flannery had been exaggerating when he said that other people in town were annoyed with Madigan for telling Fisher the truth. It was none of their affair, after all. It almost seemed as if Flannery, and the others if it were true, wanted to participate in something with which they had no business getting involved. It was almost like they were jealous that it had been Madigan, not them, who had been shot at.

He knew Flannery well enough to discount some of what he said, but if Flannery felt that way, then it was just possible others felt the same. For the moment, all Madigan wanted was to forget about the shooting, get the horses to Fort Peterson, and sleep for a week. When he woke up, he'd deal with the attempt on his life, if there was anything to be dealt with by then. The truth was that if Matt Fisher hadn't caught the man by now, he wasn't likely to. The horses were probably long gone, in any case. What worried him was leaving Sarah alone while he made the drive. Even if he rode all day, there was no way he could make the trip back in fewer than two days, with three days there, at a minimum, he was looking at damn near a week. Too long, he thought. Too damned long, but there wasn't anything he could do about it. Unless Sarah would agree to stay with Matt Fisher and his wife while he was away. He laughed out loud at that unlikelihood.

The cabin looked pretty from the top of the hill. The grass was so green, and water in the creek looked like a ragged ribbon cut from the same cloth as the sky above him. The windows caught the orange light and flashed as he cut across the hilltop, keeping the rope taut on a big bay leading the rest of the horses. Life would be good, he thought. If only it weren't so damned hard. And so damned unpredictable.

He remembered how, when he was a boy, he couldn't wait to move out of the house and be on his own. Now, when there was no home to return to except his own, he wondered what the big attraction had been. It seemed like there was nothing but work and worry. He could see his old man smiling at him from somewhere in the sky, chuckling, and leaning over to whisper to his mother, poking her with his elbow the way he did. "He's all growed up, Effie," he'd say. "Ain't he a caution. Now he knows." And that elbow would make the point one more time, until his mother slapped it away.

A picnic, it wasn't.

Sarah must have heard the horses coming, or maybe she'd seen him through the window, because she was on the porch before he was halfway down the hill. He took off his hat and waved to her, then watched as she shielded her eyes and waved back with a towel flapping in the sunlight.

He saw her leave the porch and head toward the big corral. By the time he reached the flats, she was standing by the gate, one hand resting on its top, and after turning to shoo away some of the curious stock already penned, she pulled the gate open for him to drive the last contingent inside.

He dismounted and sent his own horse outside, then hauled the bay in, getting close enough, with a little coaxing, to get the rope loose. He flipped if off the bay's head, reached out for its muzzle, and laughed when the horse backed away, tossing its mane and snorting. "Hell," he said, "even the damn animals look down their noses at me."

"Maybe you're not good enough for them," Sarah said. "My mother always had her doubts about you, too."

"Not for nothing they nicknamed you Sassy, is it?" Madigan asked, coiling the rope and heading toward the gate.

Sarah laughed, whipped the towel around his neck, and pulled him close. "Phew, you smell like an old boot," she said. "Maybe Mother was right! How about a bath?"

"That'd be nice. Long as you sit next to me. I'm afraid I might fall asleep and drown."

"You go on in and rest. I'll heat up the water."

"Good idea, but there's something I got to do, first." And he grabbed her in a bear hug.

She squirmed out of his grasp, and flicked the towel at him. "You're an animal, David. Mother *was* right." She backed away, snapping the towel at him, daring him to try to catch her again, but he was too tired to run after her, and raised his hands in surrender.

"Maybe when I get back from Peterson," he said, "I'll teach you a lesson."

He turned toward the house, and heard her skipping after him, felt one more flick of the towel on his backside, and shook his head. "My mother was right, too," he said over his shoulder.

"About what?" she asked.

"She said I should have married an older woman." He cackled all the way into the house, and only when he had the door between them did he get up the nerve to turn around to stick out his tongue.

He went on into the bedroom and started to undress. He could hear the rattle of the galvanized tub as Sarah tugged it close to the fireplace, then the bang of the screen door as she went to the well for the first bucket of water. He pulled off his boots then stripped off his sweaty clothes and lay back on the bed. With his eyes closed, he listened to the gush of water into the tub, then the bang of the door as Sarah went back for another pail.

He'd seen indoor plumbing in a hotel in Denver, and remembered taking a bath in the elaborate enameled tub and wondered what it would be like to have something that convenient in his own house. He knew there was no way he could afford it in the near future, because it meant having a water tower and a pump capable of getting the water into it, the piping, and . . . but already the list was far too long for his straitened circumstances, and he stopped counting.

The next thing he knew, Sarah was bending over him, tickling his nose with a loose thread from a towel, and he swatted at it without looking. "Quit it, Sass," he said. "I'm too tired."

"Your bath's drawn, master," she said, affecting the stilted accent of the Englishman who'd bought a dozen horses from them the previous summer. Sarah had gotten such a kick out of the retinue of servants, all seemingly dedicated to the creature comforts of an insufferable ass of a lord who had too much time on his hands and even more money.

Madigan got up with a groan. She watched him, then leaned closer to take a look at the swath of bruises down his right side. "I haven't seen that many colors on one body since Kitty Fisher got into Millie's makeup case."

"I'll bet Kitty didn't feel as sore as I do," Madigan suggested.

"She did when Millie got through with her, I'll bet." Sarah laughed, and helped him stand up. Naked, he walked toward the front room, every muscle in his body putting up an argument, and when he reached the tub, all he wanted to do was slide down into the water and go back to sleep.

He tested the temperature with a toe, then

stepped in and hunkered down. The galvanized metal was cold against his bare back, but the water was warm, and just letting it soak its heat into his aching joints was a luxury.

Sarah stood by to render whatever assistance he might need, and kept up a running chatter to keep him awake. He lathered himself from head to foot, trying with indifferent success not to slop water onto the floor. And soon he was ready for a rinse. Sarah hoisted the heavy pail and poured, the water peeling away the soapy slick that looked like the translucent outer skin of an onion.

Madigan stood up, grabbed a thick towel, and began to dry himself, rubbing so vigorously he made his skin red.

"You want to leave that skin on, David," Sarah pointed out, "it's the only thing holding you together."

He turned to her, brandishing the towel like a larger version of her earlier weapon. "Maybe you should just button your lip, Sass, if you know what's good for you."

She laughed, then asked, "Can you eat something or are you too tired for dinner?"

"I don't know. Right now, all I want to do is climb into bed. Maybe later I'll feel like eating."

She smiled. "Poor baby. You've been working so hard . . ."

"I don't mind the work. It's all the other stuff that gets to me." He wrapped himself in the towel and stepped out onto the rag rug, and headed for the bed room.

Sarah followed him in, and when he climbed under the blanket, she sat beside him. He closed his eyes, and she played with his damp hair. "Maybe if you let me come with you, it'll be a little easier, David."

Without opening his eyes, he shook his head. "Nope. You've never driven horses, Sass, especially that far. It's backbreaking work, and I'll be in the saddle twelve or thirteen hours a day for the next few days. I was thinking, though, that maybe you ought to stay with someone while I'm away."

"Like who?" she asked, tugging on his hair.

Madigan sat up and looked at her, trying to gauge her reaction. "You could stay with the Fishers. Or the Matlocks."

Sarah shook her head. "I'll be fine here. You worry too much."

"I wish I believed that."

"Why, what's the matter?"

Madigan shrugged. "I don't know. I saw Dan Flannery this morning, and he was telling me how people around here are mad I talked the sheriff into letting the Mexican go."

Sarah bristled. "What business is it of theirs?"

"That's what I said to Flannery, but you know how he is, always putting in two cents when one is too much. But . . . "

"But what? Surely you don't think I have to be afraid of our own neighbors. They might be busybodies, but they don't mean any harm."

"I know that. But all the same, if the Mexican

didn't do it, then we don't know who did. That one shot, the one that came through the window, could have hit you. Whoever it was probably wasn't shooting at you, but even so, it was too damn close a call."

"If somebody wants to shoot me, they can do it whether I'm here or at the Matlocks, David. Besides, I don't believe anyone was trying to hurt me, and neither do you." Then, as if uncertain herself, she asked, "Or do you . . . ?"

He shook his head. "No, I don't."

"Then that settles it. I'll stay here and you'll come home as soon as you can. Go to sleep." She leaned over and kissed him on the forehead.

He felt the bed shift as she stood up, and heard the bedroom door close, but it sounded a hundred miles away as he drifted off to sleep.

It was dark when he woke up. He reached out to feel for Sarah in bed beside him, then tucked the cover up around her shoulders against the chill. He was hungry, and started to slip out of bed, thinking to get something to eat without waking her. She stirred when he left the bed, and he stood stock still for a long moment, until her breathing settled back into its monotony.

In the front room, he was groping for a match when he heard one of the horses whinny. He stepped to the window and peered out into the darkness. There was just a sliver of moon, and it was difficult for him to see clearly, but he saw the horses, a huddled mass of shadow in the corral.

They were pressed against the fence, as if

something had frightened them. He thought for a moment it might be a wolf, but it didn't seem likely. It could be a bear, but that, too, was a remote possibility. At first, he didn't realize the gate was open, but when the horses started to spill out, he shouted, and ran to the mantel for his rifle.

Still naked, he flung open the front door and pushed out onto the porch. The pounding of two hundred hooves make the ground rumble as he jumped from the porch. He saw the rider then, one man, driving the horses ahead of him and he brought his rifle up, knowing that the damage was already done.

But he fired anyway, the sharp crack of the rifle sending the already frightened horses into a full gallop. The bullet narrowly missed the rider, and punched his hat, kicking it back off his head, where it balanced precariously on his shoulder for a split second until the rider grasped it by the brim.

Madigan levered another round home and tried to aim, but a pistol cracked, and the rider ducked alongside his horse as Madigan hit the ground. He lost his grip on the rifle, and by the time he got hold of it again, the man had rounded the barn and was gone.

So were the horses and three days' work.

And, just maybe, so was his future.

10

Madigan sat there in the chilly air, hugging his rifle. He heard Sarah calling to him, but he couldn't find the strength to answer her. It was easier to ignore her call, because then he wouldn't have to tell her what had happened, as if somehow things might not change if he refused to give them voice.

But Sarah came out onto the porch. "David, what on earth are you doing? Why are you sitting there like that? What's happened?"

He shook his head. "Go inside, Sassy."

"Not until you come in."

He heard the whisper of her bare feet on the boards, then felt the swish of her nightgown as she stepped down to sit beside him.

He turned to look at her then, wiping a few tears from his cheeks. "They're gone, Sass. They're all gone. Every last blessed one of them."

"David, you're not making any sense. What's gone?"

"The horses. Somebody ran them off. I saw the sonofabitch, and I shot at him. Nearly drilled him, but he got away, and took our whole life with him." He picked up the rifle, looked at it as if he'd never seen it before, then got to his feet. Twirling the rifle over his head, he let it fly, and Sarah saw it spiral off into the dark and disappear, then heard it land with a thud as it slammed into the side of the barn.

Madigan lost his footing with the exertion and slipped from the bottom step, landed hard, and collapsed in a heap. He didn't even try to get up, and Sarah moved down the steps to stoop beside him. She wrapped him in her arms and started to rock him as he sobbed. "It'll be all right, David. We'll be all right, I promise."

He kept shaking his head. "No, Sass, we're ruined. We're finished. We'll never be all right again. Every cent we have is tied up in this place, and now we're going to lose it."

She shook him then, so hard his head wobbled. "No, David. No, we won't. We'll be all right. Pull yourself together, honey."

He struggled to free himself from her grasp. When he got loose, he stood up. He was shivering, and Sarah couldn't tell whether it was from the chill or the pent-up rage. Either way, his teeth began to chatter, and she took him by the hand, tugging him toward the steps.

This time, he didn't resist, and when she got him inside, she made him sit at the table, then went to the bedroom to get him a shirt and a pair of jeans. He was sitting there, still motionless, his head in his hands, when she returned, and she leaned over to kiss the top of his head. "Here," she said, handing him the clothes. "Put these on. It's too chilly to sit around in your birthday suit."

He looked at her as if she were some sort of alien creature. "How in God's name can you take this so lightly? How can you joke at a time like this, Sarah?"

"If I don't," she said, "then who will? But somebody sure as hell has got to." She smiled, and he gave her a feeble echo in return.

She shook her head. "No, like this," she said, placing the tips of her index fingers at the corners of her mouth. She pressed the fingers toward her ears, stretching her lips into a grotesque parody of a grin, and he laughed in spite of himself.

"That looks God awful, Sass," he said.

"Well, it looks better without the fingers, but I had to show you how to do it. If you practice it, after a while, you get so you don't even need your fingers at all. The face does it all by itself. But you have to work at it."

He shivered, slipped the shirt on, and got to his feet. He slipped the jeans on, standing on one leg then the other, buttoned them up, and sat down again. Sarah filled the coffee pot and hung it over the coals, then sat down across the table from him.

She reached out her hands, and he leaned across the table to grasp them. "It'll be hard, Sass, real hard."

She nodded. "I know, David. But it's been hard before and we've managed. We'll do it again. Tomorrow, you go talk to Mr. Cartwright, tell him what happened. He'll help you work something out."

"I don't know if that's such a good idea, Sass. Cartwright knew I was counting on that army contract. But I can forget that now. I'll never get all those horses back together in time, and he'll realize that as soon as I walk through the door of the bank without the money. I know exactly what he'll say. He'll want to know why he should expect me to make payment a month or six weeks from now, when I can't make it at the end of the month. And he'll be right, too, because if I lose that contract, I can't bid on another one for six months. How in hell am I going to get that much money somewhere else? And in so short a time?"

"There must be other people who need horses beside the army. Mustn't there?" She sounded hopeful, but her face was uncertain.

"Sure, but I can't sell fifty. I doubt if I can sell half that number in six weeks."

Suppose you go to Fort Peterson and tell that Major Whatshisname . . . "

"Fletcher. Harrison A. Fletcher. And I know

you, Sass, but don't ask me what the 'A' stands for, because I don't know."

"That's beside the point," she said. "I'm being serious now, hard as that may be for you to believe. Suppose you go to the fort and tell him what's happened? Tell him someone is trying to interfere with your delivery."

"He won't give a damn. He wants the horses, and he doesn't want to hear anything about why they're not there when they're supposed to be."

"But what if you tell him ahead of time? Maybe you can convince him that it's somebody who's trying to undercut the army. For all you know, it could be true."

Madigan shook his head. "I'd rather try to make the delivery. I know it's just about impossible, but even so, I think I have a better chance of doing that than I do convincing Fletcher to give me another few days."

"How long do you need?"

"It took me three days to collect the stock last time. I suppose I can do it again in three days. Then two days to Fort Peterson. But that's two days more than I've got."

"Then the answer is simple."

"I'm glad you think so. Would you mind explaining it to me? Because I don't think it's simple at all."

"Get help, David. Ask our neighbors. You've helped them when they needed it. Now it's their turn. You need them and they'll help you, now."

"People have their own problems, Sass. They don't need to hear about mine."

"But that's what neighbors are for, David. Isn't that what you told me when Silas Hinchey's barn burned and you helped him build a new one? Isn't that what you said when Alfred Dwyer broke his leg and a bunch of you built that corral for him?"

"That was different, Sass."

"No, David, it wasn't different, and you know it. You're just being stubborn. You're so damned proud that you'd rather go under than ask for help. Isn't that so?"

He stared at her, not answering, and she bored in. "Isn't it so?" she asked again. "Aren't you too damned proud for your own good?"

He shook his head. "No, I'm not too proud, Sass, damned or otherwise."

"Good. So, you'll go into town and ask for help this morning?"

He nodded. "Yes, I'll go into town and ask for help this morning."

"Fine. I'll go with you. We'll go to the bank first and get an extension, then we'll see whether our neighbors are as charitable as I think they are. Which is only as charitable as you are with your time and your sweat. I don't think it's too much to ask, and neither will they. Now that that's settled, let's have a cup of coffee."

She went to the fireplace, got the pot, and came back to the table. She poured coffee into both cups, filling them only halfway. "I don't sleep well when I have too much coffee, and I'll need my rest if I'm going to spend the day begging," she said, laughing.

"It's not . . ."

"I'm only teasing, David."

She went back to the fireplace and set the pot on the hearth. Returning to the table, she sat down, stirred a spoonful of sugar into the cup, and sipped silently. Madigan took his black, gulping it down despite the searing heat.

When Sarah had finished her coffee, he got up from the table, waiting for her, and followed her to the bedroom. "I just hope you know our neighbors as well as you think you do, Sass," he said, turning down the lamp as she climbed into bed.

When he'd undressed and slid in beside her, she snaked an arm under his head and turned toward him. "I do, David. You'll see," she whispered.

He drifted off to sleep, still not sure she was right, but hoping he was wrong. And he didn't sleep well.

He woke early, and was up by dawn, dressed and waiting for her, breakfast on the table, by the time she joined him in the front room. Madigan played with his food, but didn't really have much of an appetite. Sarah tried to tease him out of his mood, but barely managed to get a wan smile out of him.

When she had finished her breakfast, she said, "We'll leave the dishes until we get back. I'll be ready to go in a few minutes."

"The horses are all ready," Madigan told her. "You can take your time, because the bank doesn't open until nine o'clock."

When she was ready, she came out of the bedroom, tucking the last few strands of red hair behind her ears. "All set," she announced. Madigan held the door for her, then followed her outside onto the porch. She walked down the steps and turned to wait for him. He looked at the empty corral for a long time before summoning the energy to close the door behind him.

"I know what you're thinking, David," Sarah said. "But you have to forget about it. Those horses are gone. But we'll get them back. I just know it."

He nodded dumbly, pulled the door closed, and took the steps two at a time. She was already halfway to the corral, where the sorrel and Sarah's favorite chestnut mare were waiting. She was in the saddle before he caught up to her. She rode well, and loved it, but seldom got the chance. Usually, when they went into town, they took the wagon. And there just wasn't much time for her to ride for pleasure.

Madigan mounted up, and they headed for town. He kept looking back over his shoulder as they wound up the hillside. Sarah noticed it, and tried once more to lighten his mood. "Don't worry about the house," she told him, "it'll be there when we get back. At least that's one thing they can't run off."

He laughed. "You know, Sass, the thing that

bothers me about all this is that I just can't figure out who's behind it. I mean, what does anyone gain from it all? Christ, if I had made an enemy, then maybe I could understand it as revenge or payback or something. But this . . . it's just crazy."

"Matt Fisher will get to the bottom of it, David. You just have to be patient. And I have a feeling that when he finally does figure it out, you'll be amazed that you hadn't seen it right from the beginning."

"That means the answer is right under my nose, and I just don't see it."

"Because you're not looking at it the right way, that's all. It's not what you see, it's how you look at it. Perspective. That's what you need."

"Not as much as I need money."

11

The bank wasn't open yet, and Sarah offered to wait while Madigan went to the general store to pick up a couple of things. Bill Matlock, the owner, was behind the counter when Madigan walked in. He glanced at Madigan, but didn't say anything, which struck Madigan as odd. He had known Matlock for years, and the man was about as voluble as anyone in Clarion.

Walking to the counter, Madigan said, "Morning, Bill."

Matlock looked away for a moment before answering, "Mr. Madigan."

Madigan was convinced now that something was wrong. Matlock might not feel like shooting the breeze, and that was fine, but this reception was downright chilly. The formality was something more appropriate for a minister or an undertaker. "You feeling all right, Bill?" he asked.

Once more, Matlock shifted his gaze. He played with some papers on the counter, not really reading them, but not doing anything else with them, either, except shuffle them around a little. "Why wouldn't I be?"

"I don't know. You just don't seem yourself this morning is all."

"I'm fine," Matlock snapped. "What do you want?"

"You sure you're going to sell it to me if I tell you?"

"What's that supposed to mean," Matlock demanded.

Madigan pushed his hat back on his head a little, and pawed at a lock of hair sticking out from under the brim. "Well, I guess what it means is it sounds like you don't care whether you do business with me or not. Which could be a problem, since there ain't no other store in town."

"Business. Is that what you call it when you run a tab must be three, four hundred dollars? Because I don't."

"I always pay you, you know that, Bill. What the hell's gotten into you?"

"I can't be giving charity to every damn deadbeat comes in here with a line of talk and a happy grin, Madigan. Now, you want something, or don't you?"

"Well, since you put it that way, yeah, I guess I

do. Three pounds of coffee and a box of Winchester .44 shells. That ought to do it."

"Cash money?"

"Actually, I thought I'd put it on my account."

Matlock shook his head. Once more, he looked away, as if he were reading a script. "No more credit. It's pay as you go. Or just go."

Madigan looked confused for a moment, but checked his pockets. He had two silver dollars and some loose change. "How much for the coffee and the shells?"

Matlock took a pencil from behind his ear and scratched some numbers on a brown paper sack, stabbing the point into it when he totaled it up. "Be three dollars and twenty cents."

Madigan fished through the change, saw that he had enough, and smacked the coins down to the countertop with a defiant slap. "Nice of you to leave me enough for a beer," he said. Glaring at Matlock's back, he watched while the merchant weighed the out coffee in the tray of his scale, then tipped it into a sack. He rolled the paper top closed, sending a whiff of the coffee in Madigan's direction, then tapped a fingertip along a shelf full of ammunition until he found what he was looking for.

Dropping the box of shells to the counter with a thud, he shoved it toward Madigan, then brought the bag of coffee up alongside it. "Anything else?"

Madigan shook his head. "No, I don't guess so, Bill. Sure hope you get rid of whatever the hell is eating you the next time I come shopping."

Matlock scowled, placing the coffee and bullets in the sack he used to total the purchase. "Bring cash, if you come back. And I'd like to see something against the account by the end of the month."

"Damn it, Bill," Madigan exploded. "What the hell has gotten into you?"

"Nothin', all right. Just nothin'. Just start payin' what you owe me." He turned away, pretending to take inventory of the shelves behind him.

Madigan didn't bother to say good-bye, and when he stepped onto the boardwalk and the door closed behind him with a tinkle of its bell, he turned to stare at his reflection in the dusty glass. He leaned close, as if he weren't sure he recognized himself. Through the glass, he could see Matlock watching him.

Shaking his head, he backed away from the glass and headed back toward the bank. Sarah was sitting on a bench on the boardwalk, and she spotted him. He waved distractedly, trying to decide whether to tell her what had just happened. He knew it would upset her, and telling her about it would just make him angry so he thought it best to keep it to himself.

Joining her on the bench, he slapped the paper sack.

"What's that," she asked.

"Well, since we've been drinking a lot of coffee lately, I figured I'd better get us a little more."

"Good idea."

"And, since it seems like I've been doing a

lot more shooting lately, I bought a box of rifle shells, too."

She looked at him apprehensively. "David, you're not thinking of doing anything foolish, are you? I mean . . . "

He patted her arm. "Of course not. But I am getting a mite impatient. I don't like being shot at, Sass. And I like it even less when you're around. But I wouldn't know who to go after, even if I had a mind to, so . . . "

He turned around to lean against the window of the bank. Unlike the glass at Matlock's store, it was crystal clear. He could see the bank's interior, all polished wood and new furniture, and it annoyed him. It seemed like whenever he got close to getting himself in good financial shape, something always happened. But that kind of thing never seemed to happen to those who lent money, only to those who had to borrow it. It made him dread seeing Lou Cartwright, but he knew that he had to do it, no matter how unpleasant it might prove to be.

Looking up the street, toward the hill where the more fashionable homes were, he could see the sunlight sparkling on the windows, the neat, white trim looking as if the paint hadn't even dried. The bricks were bright red, the color heightened by contrast with the dark, lush green of the trees that lined the street all the way up, and the dense banks of shrubbery planted in every front yard.

In one of those homes, Louis Cartwright was

probably adjusting his suspenders or just shrugging into his suit coat. Madigan wasn't sure which house belonged to the banker, but he thought if he watched carefully, he'd see a door open and the portly banker come out to the street for the two-block walk to his office.

But he knew that seeing that would just make him angrier, and he turned away. It hurt his pride having to come to Cartwright with his hand out. He didn't like depending on the generosity of others, but that's exactly what he needed, and there was no other way to describe his situation. At least, he couldn't think of one that Cartwright wouldn't immediately paraphrase to say exactly that.

He watched the clouds for a few moments, then turned his attention to traffic at the opposite end of the street from Cartwright's home. He saw Dan Flannery tie off his horse in front of a saloon, and hoped the rancher didn't spot him. Not only wasn't he in the mood for Flannery's intrusive nonsense, but he feared that Flannery would guess why he was sitting there in front of the bank.

Hell, he thought, all I need is a tin cup, like the beggars use. He'd seen enough of that in Philadelphia and St. Louis. And the truth was, he could see himself sitting there, his hand out, his eyes never quite engaging those of the almsgivers, fearful of their pity or their contempt. But he was afraid that his future might very well be just that bleak.

His father had often told him that there was a

lot of land out west, and that there was always a place for a man with a strong back. And he could breath fresh air, not like in the mines. Madigan wasn't above working for someone else, although working for himself had made the idea harder to swallow. But he didn't know whether he could survive the shame. And he knew for sure that he would never be able to look Sarah in the eye again. No, he didn't even want to think about that possibility.

Somehow he would have to find a way to make things work. And if it meant throwing himself on the well-cushioned mercy of a man like Louis Cartwright, he would just have to do it. After all, he told himself, it wouldn't kill him. It would just feel like it. His reverie was broken by a sharp elbow in his ribs, and he heard Sarah whisper, "Here he comes."

He turned to see Cartwright just stepping up onto the boardwalk at the end of the block. The banker's watchchain glittered in the sun, and made it look as if his vest were in the process of bursting into flame. Everything about the man spoke of privilege and luxury, and pampering. Even his hair sparkled with Macassar oil, so shiny in the morning sun it looked as if he were wearing a silver helmet.

Cartwright spotted him a moment later and nodded. Not until he was within a few paces did he say anything, and then it was just, "Morning, folks. We're not open yet. Be with you in a minute."

Cartwright walked to the door of the bank,

removed a tangle of jangling keys, and sorted through them until he found the one for the lock, inserted it with a solid click, and opened the door. Up the block, two men, both of whom Madigan knew to be bank employees, were hurrying toward him. He glanced at his watch, wondering whether they were late, saw that it was still ten minutes before nine, and relaxed a bit. The last thing he wanted to do was to have to face Cartwright when he was irritated with his employees.

The two men nodded to Madigan, tipped their hats to Sarah, and went on into the bank. Cartwright closed the door almost all the way, then opened it just wide enough to poke his glistening head through the gap. "We'll be opening in a few minutes, folks," he said, then closed the door with a sharp click.

Madigan looked at Sarah. "I know what you're thinking," she said. "But don't. It's a bank. It runs on schedule. Numbers are important. Nine o'clock. Three o'clock. Those are the most important numbers of all."

Once again, he was tempted to tell her about his reception at Matlock's store. And once again he bit his tongue. "I guess," he said, sinking down on the bench a little more, then repeated, "I guess."

He turned to look through the glass again, running a finger on its squeaky clean surface, then leaned close enough to get inside the glare. He could see the two employees, one at a small desk behind a polished wooden barrier little more than knee high, but which might as well have been the Great Wall of China, if the bank wanted to keep you on the outside. The bank employee was removing an array of items from a desk drawer and placing them one by one in a neat row. The other man was behind one of the two teller windows, and by the movement of his shoulders, Madigan guessed he was counting out cash for the drawer.

At 8:59, Louis Cartwright appeared in the doorway of his office at the rear of the bank and lowered his head like a charging bull as he headed toward the front door. The latch clicked at exactly 9:00 on the bank's interior clock, and the door pulled open. Once more, Cartwright's oiled head appeared in the opening. "It's time," he said. "Come on in, David, Sarah."

Madigan got to his feet with all the enthusiasm of a condemned man, helped Sarah up, and walked into the bank. Cartwright extended a hand, and, when Madigan grasped it, the banker closed his free hand over Madigan's elbow for a vigorous shake and to impart direction. "Come on back to my office," he said.

Madigan, followed by Sarah, led the way, Cartwright bringing up the rear. They entered the office, and Cartwright stepped around them, continuing on to take a seat behind his desk.

Gesturing to a pair of chairs arranged in front of it, he said, "Take a seat, folks." And when the Madigans were seated, he smiled broadly and asked, "Now, what can I do for you folks?"

Madigan wiped his brow, feeling the first beads of sweat beginning to form, cleared his throat, and said, "It's about that note that comes due at the end of the month, Mr. Cartwright."

"Umn humnh. Is there a problem?"

"Maybe."

"Anything to do with the trouble out at your place the last few days?"

Madigan nodded. "You could say that, yes."

Cartwright leaned forward, propping his elbows on the desk. "What exactly happened out there, anyway? I keep hearing all these wild stories. I even heard you had been killed, but Matt Fisher scotched that one right quick."

"I'm not exactly sure. Someone stole some horses, then took a few shots at me. The next day he came back and tried again." Quickly, Madigan brought him up to date, thinking that if he just touched on the major points, he could get to the real business at hand, but with a small reservoir of goodwill working for him. After completing his summary, he paused, waiting for the banker to say something.

Cartwright was in no hurry. He withdrew his elbows and leaned back in his chair again. "So you won't be able to deliver on that army contract, is that the problem?"

"Not exactly," Madigan said. "I mean. I can't make the deadline, but I'm hoping to get an extension. Just a few days. That's all I need. From the army and from you."

"I see."

Do you really, Madigan wondered, and was on the verge of blurting it out. But Cartwright resumed before he could. "I'll have to think about that, Mr. Madigan."

It was no longer David, and that seemed like an ominous sign, but Madigan wasn't about to comment on the sudden formality. He contented himself with asking, "When do you think you'll know?"

"A day or two. No more than that, I wouldn't think."

"Well, can you give me some idea of how . . . "

"I really can't, Mr. Madigan. Not until I have had a chance to consider all the possibilities. I'll let you know." He stood up abruptly, and the interview was over.

12

Outside the bank again, Madigan felt as if he'd just been run over by a wagon. Cartwright had not refused to grant the extension, but he'd not really given Madigan the chance to explain why he needed it, either. It had all been so slick that he could barely understand what had happened and how. But it meant he would not know, for a day or two at least, whether there was even a point to going on.

"Why don't you wait here a minute, Sarah? I want to talk to Matt Fisher, tell him about last night."

She nodded, and took a seat on the bench. He started for the sheriff's office, the haunting thump of her nervously tapping boots echoing behind him. But when he got to Fisher's office, it was locked up tight. There was a pencilled note tacked to the door frame in Fisher's block print, saying he would be back before noon.

Madigan leaned against the dusty glass to peer inside for a moment, took a deep breath, and turned back to Sarah. Fifty yards away, he couldn't hear the tap of her boots anymore, but he could see the steady tattoo, both toes rising and falling in unison, regular as a ticking clock or a beating heart. He knew she was nervous, because she always patted her feet when she was worried about something. But she was too tough to say anything. She didn't want to add to his worries, and she would keep her concerns to herself.

"Matt wasn't there," he told her, when he was close enough. "I guess I'll have to come back this afternoon."

He stopped in front of the bench, looking at the sky for a moment. The tapping toes stopped. Then he felt Sarah slide an arm around his waist, then pat his left hip. He hugged her to him for a few seconds, and said, "I guess we might just as well head on home, Sass. We got a lot of work to do."

She bit at her lower lip, and he knew she understood just how precarious their situation had become, but she showed no sign of breaking. Instead, she gave him a radiant smile. "You might have to let me help you with the horses, after all. Maybe I can earn my keep, for a change."

Before he could respond, she stepped off the

boardwalk, circled the hitching rail, walked to her horse, and climbed into the saddle. "Come on, mister, time's a'wastin'," she said.

Madigan untied the reins to the sorrel and set one foot in the stirrup, preparing to mount, when he happened to glance toward the end of the street. A cloud of dust was heading toward town, and it was moving fast. He pointed, and said, "Look at that. I wonder what the hell is going on?"

Sarah shook her head. "I don't think it concerns us. Let's go home."

She was right, and Madigan climbed aboard the sorrel. "We have to go that way, anyhow, so I guess we'll get a look on the way out of town."

Clarion, like so many western towns, ended abruptly. Beyond the last wall of the last building on the street, there often was nothing, not a sign of civilization. You could stand with your back against that wall and not see any indication at all that a town existed. Sometimes, in a fit of optimism, a town would stake a claim for itself on the surrounding terrain, maybe poke a stick into the ground with a handpainted sign nailed to it, and claim to demark the city limits, but Clarion, Colorado Territory, was not that aggressive. It just plain stopped, and the grass began, faded a bit in the shade of the terminal building, but hanging on right up to the foundation, nevertheless.

By the time they reached the edge of town, Madigan was able to pick out the shapes of four or five riders in the cloud, but the swirling beige dust was too dense for him to recognize any of the men. "Maybe that's Matt Fisher," he said. "He left a note saying he'd be back by noon. Maybe he's a little early."

Sarah shielded her eyes to peer at the approaching riders. "Don't see any roly-poly wearing a badge."

Madigan chuckled. "Sass, don't let Matt hear you talk like that. He's about the only friend we got, seems like."

They walked their mounts another hundred yards, and by now, the faces of the men began to resolve. "That's the sheriff, all right," Madigan said. "As long as we're here, we might as well tell him what happened."

He moved his mount to one side, just off the road, waiting for the approaching riders. He could see them all clearly now. Besides Fisher, he recognized Pete Dalhousie, the part-time deputy, and two cowboys from Darren Mitchell's Rocking M Ranch. The surprise, though, was the fifth man, almost hidden by the others, who rode in a tight circle around him. It was Rivera, the Mexican settler.

When the small group got closer, Madigan could see that Rivera's hands were tied together, then tied to the saddlehorn. "Looks like they arrested him again, Sass," Madigan said. "I wonder what in hell's going on?"

He waved to Fisher, who returned the gesture curtly. The sheriff's lips were set in a grim, white line, and he touched the brim of his hat when he saw Sarah, but said nothing.

Madigan wanted to ask what was happening, but Fisher looked like he was in no mood for conversation, so he indicated to Sarah that they would follow the sheriff back into town.

The riders all stopped at Fisher's office, so Madigan and Sarah were forced to use another hitching rail, because the one in front of Fisher's office was filled by the five mounts.

As he dismounted, the sheriff said something to Dalhousie, then walked to Rivera's horse and tugged at the knots binding him to the horse. He helped Rivera down, none too gently, then turned to Madigan and waved him over. "You might as well come on in, Dave. This concerns you as much as anybody, I reckon."

Without waiting for an answer, he grabbed Rivera by the shoulder and dragged him to the boardwalk, slowing a bit to let the prisoner negotiate the step, then stood to one side while Dalhousie opened the office door and stepped inside.

Madigan followed the two cowboys into the office, and Sarah stood in the doorway, debating whether or not she wanted to go in. Madigan cocked his head toward the bench outside, and she seemed relieved as she backed out of the doorway. He saw her sit down, then turn to peer through the glass, shielding her eyes from the reflected glare until she saw him, and he smiled.

"Take him on in back, Pete," Fisher said.

"What's going on, Matt?" Madigan asked.

"Señor Rivera has bought himself a whole

passel of trouble this morning, Dave," Fisher said. "Shot two of Darren Mitchell's boys. Killed Stan Fish outright, and I don't know whether Dick Henning is gonna make it."

One of the cowhands, Larry Martin, said, "I'll tell you one thing, Sheriff. That little greaser ain't gonna make it. That's for damn sure."

Fisher turned on him. "Larry, you better bite your tongue. I don't want to hear no talk like that. Not from you, and not from anybody else. Until I sort this mess out, you stay the hell out of town. And you tell your friends the same thing. Tell 'em I'll shoot the first sonofabitch comes through that door with blood in his eye, you understand me?"

Martin grumbled. "Seems like you ought to be lookin' out for your own people, Sheriff, not some sonofabitch Mexican."

"I don't give a damn where the man's from. If he done something wrong, he'll pay. But he'll pay the way law decides, not the way some juiced up cowpoke decides. Not as long as I'm sheriff, anyhow. Now, you and Merle get on out of here. Understand. Now!"

He stepped toward Martin, put a hand on his chest, and gave him a shove. Martin stumbled backward, and Madigan had to catch him by the arm to keep him from falling. Merle Hardman said, "No need to be like that, Sheriff. Larry's just saying what everybody thinks."

"Larry don't think and neither does anybody else around here, if they believe I'm going to put up with this sort of bullshit. Now get on back home, before I clap the two of in a cell."

Hardman bobbed his head, his skinny neck throbbing, but he gritted his teeth and said nothing.

"Go on, git," Fisher said again. And he took another step toward Larry Martin. The two cowboys left, mumbling to themselves, and Fisher slammed the door closed behind them. "Damn, but I hate this kind of thing," he said.

"What the hell happened, Matt?" Madigan asked.

Fisher took a deep breath, walked to his chair, and collapsed into it before exhaling. "Near as I can figure," he said, some of Mitchell's boys decided to pay a little visit to Señor Rivera this morning. Like I said, the Mex shot two of 'em. But it sounds to me like he had good reason. He says they were threatening him and his wife. Says he asked them to leave, but they wouldn't budge. He went inside to get his gun, and one of them threw a rock through his front window, landed in the cradle, damn near hitting his youngest kid in the head. He come out with his rifle to find Stan Fish sprinkling coal oil on the wall of his barn."

"But why? What the hell do they have against him?"

"They don't have nothing against him. Except they think it was him stole your horses and Flannery's beeves. I made a mistake bringing him in when I did. I shoulda knew better, but I was so damned sure it was him, I jumped the gun. Now, everybody thinks he's guilty. They don't know for sure of what, but that don't matter. The fact that he's a Mexican don't help him none, neither."

"Did you tell them he wasn't the one took my horses?"

"Hell, yes, I told 'em. I told everybody who asked me about it. But they all go sit in some damned saloon and get to talkin'. Next thing you know, somebody decides he's gonna be a big man, teach the Mex a lesson. One thing leads to another, and you get something like happened this morning. Those men had no damn business bein' on his place. If I was Darren Mitchell, I'd fire their asses. He ain't payin' them to be no vigilantes. He's payin' them to tend his stock. That's what they should have been doin'."

"What's their story about the shooting?"

"They say the Mex opened up on them when they was riding past his house. But they're lying. I'm sure of that. I checked out the barn. There was coal oil all over the barn wall, just like he said. I don't think he'd be fool enough to do it hisself. Anyhow, I found a match on the ground, and Stan Fish had a bunch of the same matches in his pocket when they brought him in to Doc Clemmons."

"So you believe him, then?"

"Hell, yes, I believe him. But I brung him in anyhow. Mostly for his own protection. But I don't want to give those hotheads an excuse to say I ain't doin' my job, neither. Long as he's in a cell, ain't nobody gonna get to him without going through me and Pete."

He stopped, banged his hand on the desk, and sighed. "But you didn't come here just to ask me about that, did you?" he asked.

Madigan shook his head. "No, I didn't. Somebody run off my horses last night."

"Jesus!"

Madigan told him about the raid, and Fisher listened intently. "I'm convinced now that somebody is trying to ruin me. But I don't know who or why."

"You ain't gonna make that deadline, are you?"

"Not a chance."

"Just could be that's what's behind all this, you know that?"

"I've been wondering about it, yeah. But something else is going on. I was in Matlock's General Store this morning, and Bill acted like a real bastard. I been doing business with him for five, six years, and you'd have thought he'd never seen me before. Wouldn't sell me anything on account. And he told me I better start paying up what I already owe him."

"Don't pay Bill no mind. I know what's going on with him. People around town are talking about how you're gonna lose the ranch, and he's worried he ain't gonna get paid. Plus, a lot of big mouths are flapping their gums about how you got the Mex off. It ain't nothing but whiskey talk. And Bill, well, he ain't one to buck the crowd, you know?"

"The thing is," Madigan said, "he's maybe

right to be worried. I don't make that deadline, and I don't make my bank payment. The bank takes the ranch, and I'm finished."

"You talk to Lou Cartwright about an extension?"

Madigan nodded. "He says he'll think about it."

Fisher rubbed under his chin, his callused fingers rasping on his whiskers. "Tell you what," he said, his voice higher pitched from the strain of his tautened neck muscles. "I'm about convinced that all this has something to do with stopping you from making that deadline. I got a hunch about something, and I got to go to Fort Peterson to check it out. I know the post commander, Colonel Winslow, pretty good. I was in his unit during the war. Course, he wasn't a Colonel then, just a First Lieutenant. Maybe I can get him to give you some extra time. That tightassed Major won't go against him if he says it's okay. How much extra time you need?"

Madigan shrugged. "I don't know . . . a week, I guess."

"I'll see what I can do. But I want you to do me a favor in the meantime."

"What's that?"

"I want to deputize you. It'll take me a couple of days to get over to Peterson and back. Pete's gonna need some help until I get back. I don't want nothing to happen to Señor Rivera in the meantime. And there ain't nobody else I can trust."

"Hell, you get me that extension, I'll give you a year for nothing."

"Careful, Davey. I just might take you up on that." Fisher laughed. "I'm leaving around noon. Can you get Sarah home and be back here by then?"

"Sure thing."

13

Matt Fisher was sitting at his desk when Madigan returned. It was eleven thirty. "You're early, Dave," the sheriff said. "Must be you got an interest in this damned business." He laughed, but Madigan didn't feel like joining in.

"How long you figure to be gone, Matt?" he asked.

"I'm bringing a spare horse. I figure I can get there in one day, if I push it. If I do the same thing coming home, I should be back late tomorrow night."

"You sure you want to go that hard? It's nearly a hundred miles to Fort Peterson."

Fisher looked at him incredulously. "Hell, I

don't want to go at all. But," he tapped his skull for emphasis, "I got a few things perkin' up here, and the sooner I see what's what, the better for everybody concerned."

"You want to tell me about it?"

Fisher shook his head. "No, I do *not* want to tell you about it. What I got is a hunch and a few guesses. That makes for very thin ice. But it also makes for decent law enforcement, so I'll just sit on my little hunch and those tiny guesses and see what happens. You going to be all right here?"

Madigan nodded. Tapping a canvas bag draped over his shoulder, he said "Me and Pete will have plenty of coffee and a new deck of cards. What else do we need?" He dropped the bag onto the seat of a chair, then sat on the chair next to it.

"You might pray a little, for luck."

Madigan laughed this time. "If it weren't for bad luck, I wouldn't have no luck at all, Matt. But then again, I didn't know the good Lord was in the habit of answering prayers. Been a long time since I folded my hands."

Fisher stood up, bent over to grab a pair of saddle bags leaning against his desk, and headed for the door. "Walk me out," he said.

The sheriff stepped off the boardwalk, dropped the saddlebags in place, and tied them down. Next to his horse was a bay, already saddled. Fisher mounted up. "Hand me that tether, will you, Dave?" he asked.

Madigan unhitched the follow horse and handed the lead rope to Fisher.

Fisher nodded his thanks. "Pete's up the street, getting some lunch. He'll be here in fifteen minutes or so."

"No problem."

"Look, I hope there ain't no trouble while I'm gone. But if there is, it'll be late, probably after dark. The kind of man wants to string somebody up, usually he's got to get a snootful of whiskey first. And he don't much like the light of day for his business. Long about sundown, you look sharp. And make sure one of you is awake at all times."

"We'll be all right, Matt. You just be careful. It's a long ride to Fort Peterson. And there's Crow, Cheyenne, and Sioux to look out for."

"I'll be fine. I spent four years in the cavalry, Fort Laramie, Fort Kearney. Spent a whole year with Crook in Arizona. You want to worry about Indians, you worry about Apaches. Those buggers are . . . well, never mind. I can read sign, and I ain't reckless, so . . . " He shrugged.

"Be careful, all the same."

"*You* be careful. I'd rather face a Sioux war party than a lynch mob, any day of the week. I put out the word that you been deputized. You got a gun, and you know how to use it. The thing is, you got to be willing to use it. And the man you're staring down has to know that right off. Let him know and, nine times out of ten, you don't even have to pull it. But I don't want you to take any chances. You even think you're being threatened, you shoot. Understand me?"

Madigan nodded. "I think you're overreacting, but . . ."

Fisher cut him off. "That's especially important with a mob. You'd be surprised what happens when you put a bullet in some loudmouth. Mobs go the way the wind blows. Long as some big mouth fool is whippin' them up, they'll keep comin'. They see him on the ground with a bullet in his leg, they're like smoke. The wind shifts, and they're gone." He snapped his fingers. "Like that." Then he added, "Usually, anyhow."

He turned his mount and looked over his shoulder. "See you tomorrow night, if everything works out."

Madigan waved, and watched him head out of town, then climbed back onto the boardwalk and dropped onto the bench. He saw Pete Dalhousie coming toward him, and waved. Pete returned the wave, and broke into a trot. He was puffing when he reached the bench. "Sorry I'm late. Had a bitch of a time getting out of the Arrowhead. Everybody's pulling my shirt, wanting to know what's happening with Rivera."

"What'd you tell 'em?" Madigan asked.

"Told 'em he was being held for a few days, at least until Sheriff Fisher got back. That seemed to satisfy them. For now, anyways. You eat yet?"

Madigan nodded. "Had something at home before I rode in."

"Well, what we got starin' us in the face is forty-eight hours of the most boring time you ever spent in your whole damned life."

"I sure hope so," Madigan said.

Pete laughed. "Me, too. Lots of coffee and poker. Not much sleep, and nerves twitchin' like hot snakes the whole damned time. I sure hope Matt knows what he's doin'."

"What *is* he doing?"

Dalhousie shrugged. "Damned if I know. I been with him four years. And I seen him like this once or twice. He gets a bug, he don't let go. Not ever. And he's got a bug over this, for damned sure. Thing made him mad, I think, was that shooter almost hitting your wife. Then, when Mitchell's boys almost hit that Mexican kid with the rock, he went over the edge. He always says if two grown men with guns want to shoot each other, that's fine by him. It's when innocent folks get in the way that things get ugly. And that's when he gets mad."

"He's a good man."

"Damn straight. Matt Fisher's the best. Anybody can get to the bottom of this mess, it's him. I just hope the worst is over." He slapped his knees as he leaned forward, ready to stand up. "Listen, maybe you ought to go on inside and get some shuteye. There's a cot in the back room. If you want, you can use a bunk in one of the empty cells. Come midnight, we'll both be proppin' our eyes open with matchsticks as it is."

Madigan got up from the bench. "Maybe I will go on in. It wouldn't hurt to get some rest." He entered the office, got the cell-block key from its peg, and opened the heavy metal door. To be on the safe side, he brought a Winchester with him, grabbing it from a rack, and checking to make sure it was loaded before dropping the key ring back on its peg.

The cell block was a mass of contrasting light and shadow. Brilliant sun poured in through the small, high window in each of the three cells, but the thick, dark stone walls seemed to soak it up. Shadows sat on the floor like pools of dark water. He entered the first cell, leaned the rifle in the corner, and sat down on the bunk. The straw mattress rustled under his weight, and a faint stink of beery vomit swirled up around him.

He glanced into the middle cell, where Francisco Rivera lay on his bunk, his arms folded behind his head, staring at the ceiling. Madigan wanted to say something to the man, but didn't know how to begin. He felt somehow responsible, as if the Mexican had gotten sucked into something that really had nothing to do with him.

But Rivera never looked at him, and he contented himself with leaning back against the wall, ignoring the jabs of the rough stone into his shoulder blades and the back of his head. His wounded arm still bothered him a bit, and he rested it in his lap. To kill the stink, he rolled a cigarette and lit it. Before putting the fixings away, he looked at Rivera again. "You want a cigarette, Señor?" he asked.

Without taking his eyes off the ceiling, Rivera said, "What I want is to go home to my family, Señor."

"I don't blame you."

"Somebody does, Señor," Rivera said, turning his head and looking at Madigan for the first time. "Somebody does."

"Look, Rivera, for what it's worth, I believe you when you say you didn't take my horses or those cows. I believe you had nothing to do with shooting at me, or running off my horses. Sheriff Fisher believes you, too."

"I have a bill of sale for those cows, Señor. That should prove I did not steal them. But I can't have a bill of sale for horses I did not buy and do not have. How can I prove that I did not take something that no one can find?"

He sat up now, his boots thudding on the cement floor. "I would like a cigarette, yes," he said. He got to his feet and walked to the bars separating the two cells. Madigan got to his feet and handed the tobacco pouch through the bars. Rivera rolled a cigarette, passed the pouch back, and exchanged it for a box of matches. Lighting the cigarette, he exhaled the smoke in twin streams, then passed the matchbox back to Madigan.

He sucked on the cigarette until it was just a nub, its glowing tip almost flush with his fingers. After one last drag, he dropped it to the floor and ground it under his toe. "You know, Señor, I bought those cows from the man I shot this morning. The one they called Fish."

Madigan was stunned. "What?"

Rivera nodded. "That is not the name he put on the paper, but he is the man."

"Did you tell that to the sheriff?"

Rivera shook his head. "No. What difference would it make? He wouldn't believe me, and I cannot prove it. And the man Fish cannot say anything now. Why did he lie to me, Señor? And why did he try to burn my barn?"

"I wish to hell I knew, Rivera. God as my witness, I wish to hell I knew."

"Why did the *jefe* arrest me, Señor Madigan? I only tried to protect myself and my family. I never hurt anyone. I never stole anything. And until this morning, I never shot a man in my life. But I am treated like a criminal."

"You're not in here because Sheriff Fisher thinks you're a criminal, Señor Rivera."

"Then why?"

"Because the sheriff is worried that someone might try to hurt you."

Rivera shook his head as if that was logic beyond his comprehension. "Someone tries to hurt me, to burn my barn, and *I* am the one in jail? In Mexico, as bad as it is sometimes, it is still the criminals who get put in jail. Are there so many criminals here that it is easier to put the good men inside and leave the criminals outside?"

"No, of course not. But people around here are upset. Someone stole cattle from Dan Flannery. Someone stole horses from me, then ran off a herd I was getting ready to drive to Fort Peterson. Someone also shot at me. Three times. Folks are mad, and they're looking for someone to take it out on. You're the one they settled on, that's all.

And Matt wants to see to it that nothing happens to you until he has a chance to find out who's responsible for all of that."

"And while I am in here, there is no one to look after my family."

"They'll be all right. If you want, I can ask someone to look in on them."

Rivera shook his head. "No, I don't think so. I think the less we have to do with people the better off we are. We tried to make a life here, but I don't think that will be possible. I think we should got back to Mexico. If the sheriff wants, I will leave right away, as soon as he lets me out. Then he can have the cell for the men who stole the cattle and your horses. If *you* let me out right now, Señor, I will leave tonight."

Madigan shook his head. "Sorry, but I can't do that, Señor Rivera. You wouldn't be safe. And it's just possible the sheriff might need you as a witness."

"I saw nothing that I did not already tell you, Señor. I know nothing I have not told you."

"Maybe so. But I still can't let you out. Besides, maybe you know something you don't realize you know. Maybe you saw something that doesn't mean anything to you but might mean something to the sheriff. If he finds the men responsible for the rustling and the shooting, he's going to need help proving it. You might be able to do that."

Rivera shook his head. "I don't think so, Señor." He turned away then, and walked back to his bunk. He sat down, started to say something, then changed his mind and lay back on the mattress. A moment later, and his hands were back behind his head, and he was staring at the ceiling again. If Madigan didn't know better, he would have been tempted to think Rivera had never moved at all, that he had imagined the entire conversation. The only proof it had happened was the crushed cigarette butt on the floor of Rivera's cell.

He sat on the bunk, rolled onto his side, and closed his eyes. Maybe, he thought, after a little sleep, things would make more sense.

14

When Madigan woke up, it was dark outside. He saw the bars surrounding him and for a moment was disoriented. He sat up, rubbing his eyes, and looking around him, tried to remember why he was in jail. As his mind cleared, he sighed with relief, and almost laughed when he saw the rifle in the corner and the open door to the cell. Everything was wrapped in shadow, except for the oblong of orange light spilling through the cell-block door from the front office.

He looked into the next cell, squinting, and barely saw Rivera, now curled in a ball on his bunk, a ragged, blue blanket wrapped around him. For a moment, Madigan thought the Mexican might be dead. He was so still. Listening, Madigan heard no breathing, no snoring, and the blanket was virtually motionless.

He walked to the bars separating the two cells and pressed his face against them. He still heard nothing, and the blanket still appeared to be motionless. He was about to call to Rivera when the man moved, turning his back and sighing. Relieved, Madigan grabbed his rifle from the corner and went out to the front office.

Pete Dalhousie was sitting at Matt Fisher's desk, playing solitaire. He looked up, a broad grin on his face. "My God," he said, "I've heard of the sleep of the just, but you must be a god-damned saint. I looked in on you one time, you was like a rock. A loud one, I have to admit, but, man, you was still as a corpse."

"You should have wakened me, Pete."

"No need. Ain't nothing happening. The street's quiet, and when the sun went down, I just closed the front door and put the latch on. Ain't nobody even walked by the front of the place, at least not that I saw."

"You want to get a little sleep?"

Dalhousie shook his head. "Not yet. Maybe later. What I'd like to do is get something to eat."

"Go ahead, then. I'll hold down the fort."

Dalhousie nodded. "You want me to bring you something back?"

"If it's no trouble."

"No trouble at all. I figure to get some chicken and rice from Mabel's Place. You ever eat there?"

"Once or twice."

"I don't know what the hell she puts on her chicken, but it's the best damn chicken I ever tasted. Some rice with red and black beans, a touch of jalapeño sauce and, man, oh man. 'Course, a little beer sharpens it right up, too, but I ain't going to drink until Matt gets back. He'd have my hide if he found out I was hoisting while he was out of town. Besides, a beer'd put me right out."

He got to his feet and stretched. "Be back in about a half hour. Keep the door locked, if you want. But whatever you do, don't let nobody in you don't know. And if anybody you *do* know comes by, send him packin'. Thing like this, you don't know who to trust so you're better off trustin' nobody. And I do mean nobody. Hell, even if Sarah comes in, you'd best look at her cross-eyed, just to be sure."

"You make it sound like real fun, Pete."

"Naw. The fun starts when you get a bunch of yahoos out front danglin' a rope and belchin'. That's when you know it's gonna be a long night. Lord willin' we won't have to deal with anything like that. The thing of it is, half the time you got to shoot somebody to break up a mob. And more often than not, it's somebody you know."

"I don't know if I'm ready for that."

"Nobody ever is. Most times, it's some guy you play horseshoes with, some guy bought you a drink a time or two. But when he gets in a mob, he ain't the same guy. The onliest thing about it is, next day, when everybody's sober, you still remember how you had to plug him. If he lives, he probably don't ever talk to you again. And if he don't, then you got to wonder about his friends, what they'll do the next time they have a few drinks and start talkin' about what a nice guy old Al or Mike or Andy was. And what a damn shame it was what happened to him."

Madigan laughed. "Sounds to me like a hell of a way to make a living, Pete."

"Part-time is all I could take, Dave. Believe me. Part-time is plenty. Anyhow, let me get out of here. I'll bring back some chicken, rice, and beans for you."

"See you in a bit, then. Listen, let me give you some money."

Pete waved him off. "I got it, Dave."

"Bring enough for Rivera, too, will you?"

Dalhousie looked surprised, but he nodded. "Whatever you say, Dave."

As soon as Pete left the office, Madigan slid the bolt home. He felt a little silly doing it, because the front door was wood and glass, and anybody who wanted to get through it wouldn't be stopped by a fifty-cent bolt. But at least it meant he'd have warning if anybody tried the knob or wanted to burst in on him.

He debated pulling down the shades on the door and the front window, but decided that he'd rather be able to see the boardwalk and a bit of the street, not that he could see a whole lot. Clarion was not exactly a metropolis, and streetlights were far down on the list of improvements the town needed. And to make matters worse, the glass of the large window was streaked with dust and dirt.

He gathered Pete's cards and stacked them, then shuffled them three or four times, on the last pass trying a fancy riffle he'd seen a gambler in St. Louis do with one hand. But when the cards spurted all over the desk top, he gave it up, gathered the cards again, and shuffled twice more before laying out a game of solitaire.

It brought him back to his childhood, in Pennsylvania. He'd played solitaire almost every day, waiting for his father to come home from the mines, slapping the cards down harder and harder as it got later and later. They played poker together, he, his father, and his brothers, Patrick and Brian. But only when Patrick Madigan Senior wasn't too tired, which wasn't often.

Everyday, the cards would be laid out, the four hands dealt around sundown in winter, a little later in the warmer months, when the men stayed in the coal seams longer. He never understood why light made a difference when the men worked so far underground, and no matter how many times his father explained that mining was more than lying on your back, hacking at the coal with a pick, that it had to be brought up, that it had to be run through the tipple, that there were things to be done to the great hunks of gleaming black rock that could only be done above ground, and the more daylight you had the more you could do.

He resented it when his father was too exhausted to play. It always made him feel selfish, but on those long days, when his father fell asleep over a straight flush, too tired to know he had it or, more likely, too kindhearted to play it against his own boys, Madigan relished the occasional victory too much to care. Now, slapping the cards down, thinking of cheating, the way he always did when faced with the brutal randomness of solitaire, he wished he had been more understanding, wished that he had let his father win more often. But Patrick Madigan Senior was long dead, and it was far too late for that sort of reparation now.

He lucked out with two kings showing, set them aside, flipped the cards beneath them, and looked at the face-up cards for a queen. There was none, and he turned the first card in the stack, a black three, had a red four on which to place it, then took a black two from one of the seven piles.

Scrutinizing the cards again, he heard a thump on the boardwalk outside, glanced at the window, thinking it was too soon for Pete Dalhousie to be returning. The dusty glass looked smeary in the orange light of the single kerosene lamp, and he couldn't tell whether he saw a shadowy silhouette through the glass or just the contrast of light and dark where the lamplight struck it. There was no movement, but he set the cards down, starting to get up from the chair.

Another thump, this one more distant,

brought him to his feet. He reached for the Winchester leaning against the side of the desk, and brought it up, reaching for the lamp and turning down the wick to extinguish it. He walked to the door on tiptoe, stopped with his ear pressed against the glass of the door and listened. He heard another thud, this one gritty, as if something had fallen into the street, then rapid footsteps racing along the side of the jailhouse. And he knew then what was happening without really seeing it clearly. Someone was after the prisoner.

Racing to the cell-block, he shouted, "Rivera, turn off your lamp!"

He burst through in time to see the startled prisoner sitting up on his bunk. The lamp was on the floor across the cell, and Rivera started to get up, his face confused. "Get the lamp!" Madigan shouted.

Rivera, galvanized by the shout, stumbled from the bunk and across the stone floor of the cell. Madigan saw movement at the high window and skidded to a halt, bringing his rifle to bear as the barrel of a pistol poked through the bars. Madigan couldn't see anything but the gun barrel and a hand. As he aimed, he realized he'd forgotten to chamber a round, worked the lever, and then tried to sight. The pistol fired and the bullet sparked on the floor, narrowly missing Rivera and ricocheting through the bars and slamming into the wall behind Madigan.

"Put it out, dammit!" Madigan yelled.

Rivera got to the lamp, knocking it over in his haste. The glass chimney shattered on the stone floor, but the Mexican righted the base, then twisted the wick down. In the sudden darkness, the pungent scent of kerosene began to well up.

It was too dark to see clearly now, but the pistol fired again, a bright spurt of flame outlining the bars for a split second. This shot, too, missed, and Madigan turned and raced back through the cell-block doorway and wrenched the latch of the front door aside, then jerked the door open and ducked out onto the boardwalk, keeping to a crouch in case the gunman had an accomplice, just waiting for Madigan to do something foolish.

He steeled himself for the impact of a bullet or the bark of a gun, but it was silent. He ran to the end of the boardwalk, jumped to the ground, and started down alongside the jail. He heard the pistol again, then footsteps racing away.

As he reached the corner he slowed, leaning forward to peer along the backs of the buildings. He saw a tall, shadowy figure sprinting away. For an instant, it was starkly lit by light spilling from the back room of the Arrowhead Saloon, but the figure was there and gone so quickly, Madigan saw nothing more than the back of a man dressed in jeans and a denim shirt. He didn't even catch the color of the man's hair, because he wore a stained, gray Stetson, like a hundred other ranch hands in Clarion.

On impulse, Madigan started after the gunman and ran a few yards along the back of the jailhouse. Then, remembering he'd left the office door open, and that Rivera was alone, trapped in his cell, he stopped so abruptly he almost lost his balance, and ran back to the front.

He saw Pete Dalhousie ambling along the boardwalk, a package in his hand, and he shouted, "Pete, hurry up!"

Dalhousie looked startled, then broke into a run, his boots thumping on the boardwalk as Madigan ran through the office and into the cell-block. "Rivera, you all right?" he called.

"*Sí*, I am all right, Señor Madigan." The voice sounded distant, even faint, and Madigan still wondered whether the prisoner had been wounded.

"Were you hit?"

"No. Just scared, Señor." This time, the voice sounded cold and stilted, muffled somehow, but in the darkness, he couldn't see. Then Madigan heard footsteps and turned just as someone ran into the office, tightening his grip on the Winchester.

"Hey, what happened to the lights? What the hell's going on? Dave, you there?" It was Pete, and Madigan relaxed.

Madigan moved to the doorway. "I'm back here, Pete."

"What happened to the lights?"

Dalhousie set his package down with a rustle of paper, then moved cautiously toward the cell-block doorway. Madigan stepped out into the front office, bumped against a chair as he groped for the edge of the desk. Finding the lamp, he reached into his pocket for a match, removed the chimney and struck the match. When he could see again, he raised the lamp wick and lit it, waiting to make sure it caught before replacing the chimney.

"Somebody just tried to kill Rivera," he said.

"What?" Dalhousie looked confused, his eyes clinched, the leathery skin of his cheeks suddenly filled with wrinkles. "Are you serious?"

"Never been more serious in my life, Pete."

"Who was it? What happened?"

Madigan told him as much as he knew, which was precious little. When he was finished, he said, "I think we got to move him."

"Move who, Rivera?" Dalhousie asked.

Madigan nodded. "We can't leave him in there like that. He's trapped like a rat."

"Where the hell can we move him?"

"What about the back room? You said there's a cot there. Is there a window?"

Dalhousie shook his head. "No, no window and, yeah, there's a cot, but . . . "

"Pete, we're supposed to keep him alive until Matt gets back. That's all I care about right now. We have a better chance of doing that if nobody can get to him from the outside. If anybody gets past us, he's a dead man whether he's in the spare room or his cell, so what's the difference? We'll have to stay awake all night, and he's not going to go anywhere anyhow."

Dalhousie took a deep breath. "I suppose you're right . . . "

"You bet your ass I am."

15

Madigan walked back into the cell-block, carrying the lamp. Rivera was huddled on the floor up against the wall directly beneath the window. His knees were up and his head bent, as if he were trying to curl himself into a ball. Even when Madigan turned up the lamp, the prisoner didn't move.

The jangle of the keys made Rivera quiver, as if the least noise were something to be feared. Even when Madigan inserted the key into the lock, Rivera ignored him. The loud click of the bolt when Madigan turned the key echoed off the stone walls. It sounded like a hammer falling on a dud round, and Madigan instinctively glanced toward the window over Rivera's head.

Opening the door, Madigan stepped inside and walked toward Rivera, squatting down in front of him and setting the lamp on the floor. The smell of the spilled kerosene was sharp in the air, and when he balanced himself with one hand on the floor, Madigan could feel the greasy slick on the cold stone. "Señor Rivera," he said. "It's going to be all right. Come on now, we're going to move you to another room."

Rivera shook his head without looking up. "It doesn't matter, Señor Madigan. Someone wants to kill me. If he tries hard enough, he will manage to do it."

"Not as long as I have anything to say about it, he won't."

"You can do nothing, Señor."

Madigan reached out to pull Rivera's hands away from his face. "Look at me, Francisco. Look up, dammit!"

But Rivera just burrowed down more securely among his limbs. He looked like a frightened animal trying to protect itself from something it could not see but knew was somewhere close by. He was trembling now, and Madigan suddenly felt sorry for him.

"Francisco, come on, now. It'll be all right. Pete and I will protect you. No one is going to hurt you."

Rivera still refused to look up. And Madigan shifted his position, kneeling in the kerosene slick to bring more leverage to bear as he tried to force Rivera to uncoil. "Listen to me, you can't stay here. If that man comes back, he might not miss you again. With the windows in here, you're an easy target. Is that what you want? Do you want to sit here and wait for him to come back? Because if that's what you want, then, dammit, you go right ahead and sit there."

Rivera said nothing, and Madigan was getting angry. "Look," he snapped, "suppose he does come back. Suppose he shoots you. Who will look after your family, then?"

For a moment Madigan thought he might have gotten through to the frightened man, but he remained tightly curled, and Madigan stood up, disgusted. "Pete," he called. "Come on and give me a hand, will you?"

He turned toward the cell-block door waiting for the deputy to answer him. He heard footsteps in the outer office, then saw a shadow on the floor. Pete appeared in the doorway, carrying a rifle. "What's up, Dave?" he asked.

"I can't get this sonofabitch to stand up, but I'll be damned if I'm gonna leave him here. Help me carry him into the spare room, will you?"

"Sure thing." Dalhousie leaned his rifle against the inside wall and walked to the cell. Madigan positioned himself on one side of Rivera, and Pete took the other side. Sliding one hand behind the prisoner, they locked them around each other's wrist, then did the same in front, by forcing their hands under Rivera's knees.

"On three," Madigan said. "One . . . two . . . three . . . "

They straightened up. Rivera was not that large a man, but he was not cooperating, and he made a heavy burden as they moved toward the cell door. "Sumbitch, we ought to drop him on his ass, see if that don't straighten him out a little," Dalhousie grunted. "Seems like an awful lot of trouble to go to help a man who don't want to be helped."

Madigan said nothing as he turned and backed through the cell door. They staggered into the front office, skirted the desk, and bumped through the doorway into the back room. The cot was against the back wall, and when they reached it, they lowered Rivera none too gently.

The prisoner still hadn't moved of his own volition. Now, he turned on his side, still tight as an armadillo, his front side toward the wall. Madigan grabbed a blanket, snapped it open, and tossed it carelessly over the huddled mass.

"I guess that about does it," Dalhousie said. "He wants something to eat, he's gonna have to move his ass and get it, because I'll be damned if I spoon feed the sonofabitch." He glared down at Rivera and added, "You hear that amigo? You want to eat, you get your ass out front and get it yourself."

He spat on the floor in disgust, rubbed the hawker into the dust with the toe of one boot, and stomped out front. From the front office, he called, "Come on, Dave, dinner's gettin' cold."

"Be right out, Pete."

Madigan stooped down beside the cot, staring

at Rivera's back. "Look," he said, "Francisco, I know you're scared. Hell, I'm scared, too. But we can't neither one of us crawl into a hole and die. We do that, and it's the same thing as letting that bastard shoot us dead. I won't let that happen to either one of us, if I can prevent it. But it'd be a whole lot easier if you pulled your own weight. Now, if you want, I'll give you a gun to keep in here. I can't let you go, but I'll go that far. Maybe you'll feel safer then, I don't know. I guess I can see why you might."

Rivera moved on his own for the first time. He turned his head, then rolled onto his back, and looked at Madigan, his face frightened, confused, his eyes darting back and forth as if shadowy enemies lurked somewhere behind Madigan. "You would do that, Señor Madigan? You would give me a gun?"

Madigan nodded. "Yeah, sure. I would do that."

"Why?"

"Because I think you and me have the same enemy. Because I think whoever it is, wants you dead for some reason that neither you nor I understands, just like I don't understand why somebody wants me dead, or ruined financially. Or maybe both. Maybe the simplest way to put it is to say I'll give you the gun because I trust you."

Rivera looked at Madigan a long time before responding. When he did, the answer took Madigan by surprise. "Señor, you are a good man. For a long time I din't think that I . . . " he choked up then, and turned away.

Madigan was embarrassed by the display of emotion. Clearing his throat, he said, "Listen, Francisco. When this is all over, and it will be over soon, I promise you, you and I are going to go to the Arrowhead and tie one on."

"¿Qué?"

"Get drunk, Francisco, *borracho*. We are going to drink a snootful of tequila and whiskey and teach each other songs. We will sing until they throw us out into the street, and then we'll walk a few doors and find another saloon and do it all over again. How about that?"

Rivera smiled, wiped at his cheeks, and said, "If my wife let's me, Señor, I would like that."

Madigan straightened up. "Come on, let's get something to eat. Pete brought us some food back and I'm starved."

Rivera sat up then, lowered his feet to the floor so gingerly it seemed as if he wasn't sure it was there at all. He slapped his boots on the wooden floor once, then again, and stood up. "You are a good man, Señor Madigan. I thank you."

"You don't have to thank me, Francisco, because I ain't doing anything I think you wouldn't do for me if the shoe were on the other foot."

Madigan led the way out front. Pete was playing solitaire again. He looked up at Rivera, frowned for an instant, then said, "So, you got the little armadillo to straighten up, did you?"

Rivera laughed, and Pete looked surprised.

"You're in a good mood all of a sudden, amigo."

Rivera nodded. "*Sí*, I am."

Pete got up from the desk, mounded the cards, then straightened them into a neat stack. "You fellers might as well sit down and eat. I'll keep watch for a while." He picked up his rifle and walked to the window to pull down the shades. "Might as well make it as hard for them bastards as we can," he said. "If they want to shoot me, they're gonna have to guess where I'm at."

Then he kicked a chair toward the wall and sat down, tilting it back and balancing the rifle across his bent knees. Madigan uncovered the food. The smell of chicken filled the room, and the sharp tang of salsa made him realize just how hungry he was.

Dalhousie said, "Matt keeps a Bowie knife in the bottom drawer of the desk. You can split the bird with it. That's all he uses it for, anyhow."

Madigan opened the drawer, found the knife and removed it from its sheath. He used the heavy blade to split the roasted chicken right down the middle, handed half to Rivera, then wiped the knife on his jeans and returned it to the sheath and the drawer.

Pete had also brought two bottles of beer, and Madigan used the edge of the desk to knock the caps off. He passed one bottle to Rivera and set the other down beside the plate of rice and beans. He used a fork to portion the vegetables, scooping half onto the plate with the rest of the chicken. Rivera took the remaining half and dropped his chicken beside his share of the rice and beans.

"You know," Dalhousie said, while the two men started to eat, "this whole damned thing don't make any sense to me."

"Me either," Madigan said, gnawing ravenously on a chicken wing.

The deputy went on. "I mean, why shoot Rivera, here, if he don't know nothing?"

"It's like I told him," Madigan said, pausing to take a swig of beer, "I think Francisco knows something that he doesn't know he knows. Either that, or somebody *thinks* he does. Whichever it is, they want to make sure he doesn't tell me or Matt what it is."

"Well, I'll tell you one thing, Davey, we don't figure it out pretty soon, well . . . I wouldn't want to be in your shoes."

Madigan nodded. "I know, but what the hell can I do, Pete?"

"Well, for one thing, you . . . "

"Ssshhh! Listen!" Madigan snapped. He set down his fork and got to his feet, grabbing his rifle. The sound drifted toward them, muffled, indistinct, but decidedly ominous. It sounded like a group of men, agitated, boisterous, and heading their way. Glancing at Rivera, he said, "You better get in back, Francisco."

Rivera shook his head. "No, Señor. I am not going to hide anymore. I have done nothing wrong. I will not go into the ground like a squirrel. Not anymore."

"All right, but you stay in back of us.

Understand? And if anything happens, you get in the back room right away." He went to the gun rack and unlocked it, taking down a rifle and handing it to Rivera.

"There's bullets in the rack drawer, Davey," Dalhousie said. "I need some, too."

Madigan nodded, grabbed the drawer pull and yanked open the drawer. He took out a box of .44s and opened it, handing a dozen shells to Rivera, a handful to Dalhousie, and then pocketing a few for himself.

The racket was growing louder now, and individual voices could be picked out of the murmur, although the words were still indistinct.

"I think maybe we ought to go outside, Davey. They see us, they just might think twice about coming any further."

They could hear feet pounding on the boardwalk now, the excited babble rising in intensity as if the drumming feet were some military tattoo. Dalhousie pulled back the bolt and jerked the door open. He stepped out onto the boardwalk, Madigan right behind him.

"There they are," somebody shouted.

Dalhousie worked the lever of the Winchester, aimed at the sky and fired.

"That's about far enough, boys," he shouted.

"Where's the little greaser?" one of the rabble yelled. "Hand him over."

Madigan jerked a round home and stepped out of the doorway. "That isn't about to happen, boys," he said.

"Madigan, you sonofabitch, what the hell are sticking up for the little beaner for? You in it with him?"

This time, he recognized the voice. It was Dan Flannery.

"Dan," Madigan said, "this is not your business. It's mine, and Matt's, so why don't you just go on home and sleep it off?"

"You sayin' I'm drunk."

Madigan hesitated for just a moment. "Well, let me put it this way, Dan. You're either drink or stupid. You're a neighbor, so I hope you're drunk, because when you wake up in the morning, that'll be gone. But if you're stupid, well, sleep ain't gonna help that none."

"You shut up and get out of our way, Davey."

Madigan shook his head.

"Sorry, boys. That just ain't gonna happen."

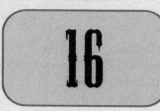

16

Madigan walked along the boardwalk until he reached the end of the sheriff's office. Behind him, Pete Dalhousie whispered, "Be careful, Dave. Don't be gettin' too close, now." Madigan nodded that he'd heard, but took another step or two.

The mob stood in a tight knot fifteen yards away. Madigan wasn't sure how many men there were, but he guessed at least a dozen. As long as they stayed together, he'd be all right, but if they started to fan out, he'd have to back up to make sure no one got in behind him.

"What the hell are you all trying to do?" he asked. "You have no business here."

"What we're tryin' to do is Matt Fisher's job,"

156

Flannery said. The remark drew a nervous laugh from the crowd, and it encouraged Flannery to go on. "Fact is, you get out of the way, and we can all go home, Davey. Twenty minutes, and this is all a memory."

"I can't, Flannery, you know that."

"Why, 'cause you been deputized? You take that seriously? If you want to know what I think . . ."

"I don't," Madigan snapped.

But Flannery was undeterred. "I think Matty Fisher left town because he knew we'd be comin'. Not that he was afraid, you understand, but because he don't care no more than a fig about that damned beaner you got locked up in the jail. Matty knows what's what. He knows he's got to live in this town, and he knows what we want."

"If you think that, you don't know Matt Fisher," Pete shouted. "You all ought to be ashamed of yourselves. Hell, I'm surprised some of you are even here. You ought to be home with your families."

Flannery rushed to cut off the deputy. "We let that greaser get away with robbin' us blind, we won't have no homes to go to. Nor no families, neither, come to that. He took something that didn't belong to him, and he's got to pay."

"You don't know that," Madigan snapped. "Look, it was my horses got run off, and I'm telling you, Rivera didn't do it."

"You keep talkin' about your horses like they

was the only thing that mattered. What about my beeves? Don't they count?"

"Rivera said he bought them, Flannery. You know that as well as I do."

"Well, he sure as hell didn't buy 'em from me. They weren't for sale no how, and I didn't get no money for 'em, neither. Here," he said, reaching into his pants and pulling one of the pockets inside out, "you see any money, Davey?"

"Rivera didn't say he bought those cows from you. He says he bought them, and that he has a bill of sale. Maybe somebody else run them off, and sold them to Rivera figuring he didn't know any better."

"You expect me to believe that?" Flannery turned to the mob. "He actually expects me to believe that. Don't that just about beat all?"

Flannery was playing to the crowd, and Madigan was worried. As long as Flannery kept them amused, they would be on his side. And they were in no mood to listen to logic. But Madigan knew he had to try.

"Listen, if I thought the man was guilty, why would I be standing here between you and him? Does that make any sense to you?"

"You could be stupid," Flannery suggested. The men laughed again, louder this time. "Could be, Davey, just could possibly be."

Madigan changed tack. "I'm telling you men to go on home before this gets out of hand. I don't want to shoot anybody, but by God, I'm here to tell you that I will if I have to."

"You ain't the only one with a gun, Davey," Flannery pointed out. "Fact is, you and Pete there are outgunned about six to one, the way I figure it. That sound like good odds to you?"

Flannery moved to his left, near the edge of the boardwalk. Madigan watched him closely, telling himself that the moment Flannery stepped into the street, he was going to shoot, and if he had to shoot Dan Flannery, that would be all right.

"Is it really worth all this, Flannery? Put yourself in Rivera's shoes. If you were he, wouldn't you want a fair trial? Wouldn't you think you were entitled to it?"

"Sorry, Davey, but I don't know how to think like no greaser. Maybe I had some of them beans and peppers they like so much, I could give it a try." The men laughed again. And Flannery grinned broadly. He was enjoying himself, and it pissed Madigan off. He felt his trigger finger getting itchy, but he didn't dare take it of the trigger, because if things got out of hand, it would happen quickly, and a split second might mean the difference between living and dying.

He wanted to back up, but knew Flannery would take that as a sign that he was winning, an invitation to move closer, and he couldn't risk it. Instead, he took a step forward. Lowering the muzzle of his Winchester until it was leveled on Flannery's gut, he said over his shoulder, "Pete, get a pencil and some paper."

"What?"

"Paper and pencil. Get it."

"What the hell are . . . ?"

"Just do it."

He heard Dalhousie's boots on the walk, and risked a glance over his shoulder in time to see Pete disappear into the open doorway to the office.

"What you gonna do, Davey," Flannery asked, "draw us a pitcher?"

Once more, loud guffaws greeted the jab, but Madigan ignored it. Flannery turned his head. "Make sure you get my good side, would you, Davey?"

"I'm hard pressed to tell you got one," Madigan said. It drew a laugh, and he felt encouraged.

He heard Pete behind him. Once more, he risked a peek over his shoulder. He nodded when Pete held up a stubby pencil and a sheet of paper. "What you want me to do, Davey?" the deputy asked.

"Write down these names, Pete. Start with Dan Flannery, and add 'rancher' after his name."

"What the hell . . . ?"

"Just do it, Pete. Trust me, I know what I'm doing. Write down Dan Flannery's name."

"Jesus, all right, whatever you say."

Madigan heard the scratch of the pencil on the rough paper. When it stopped, he said, "Got it?"

"Got it," Pete answered. "Now what?"

"Bill Matlock. Write him down, and add 'storekeeper.' " And he looked at Matlock, who seemed to be trying to melt into the crowd. "Or would you prefer something grander, Bill, like 'merchant,' maybe, or just plain old 'business-man'? That sounds a little too grand, though, not like you at all."

He heard a grumble of protest from the store-keeper, and he took a step closer to the crowd. "What's the matter, Bill? You're here ain't you?"

"Yeah, I'm here, but . . . " The merchant stopped, confused and more than a little nervous. "I don't want my name on no paper, Madigan."

"Hey, you're here, you get your name taken down. What's the matter, you ashamed?"

"Don't listen to this bullshit," Flannery barked. "He's just tryin' to scare you, that's all he's doin'. Don't pay any attention to him."

"Why should they be scared, Flannery? Are they doing something wrong?"

"Hell, no, they ain't doing nothing wrong, but . . . "

"But what?" Madigan demanded. "Go on, dammit, tell me. But what? You're here, you ought to be proud of yourselves, don't you think? I mean, all you're doing is getting ready to string up a man who can't defend himself. You have every reason to be proud. Hell, I'm surprised you didn't all bring your wives and children, let them see their husbands and daddies acting like big men. That's what you're doing, isn't it?"

"Shut up, Madigan, I'm warning you."

Flannery took a step forward, and Madigan jutted out his chin, waving the rifle a little, for emphasis. "Go on, Flannery, take another step. Go ahead."

Flannery stayed put, and Madigan said, "Paddy Collins. Then . . . what do you think, Pete, 'bartender?' 'Saloonkeeper?' Or maybe 'vendor of fine spirits.' That's what it says over the door at the Arrowhead, isn't it, Paddy? 'Vendor of fine spirits?' I kind of like that."

Collins looked uncomfortable. He stroked his mustache, and shrugged his shoulders nervously, but said nothing.

"Okay, who's next? Who else wants his name on the list? We'll probably put this in the *Clarion Herald* next Monday. It's a goddamned shame we don't have a photographer here, come to think of it." Madigan leaned toward the crowd, exaggerating his gaze as he peered at one face after another. "Wait a minute, there's the editor of the paper, Milt Henderson. Milt, you know where we can get a photographer on short notice? Be nice to have a picture of you all, don't you think? You could tack it up on the cork board you got down at the *Herald*. Shame you can't print photographs in the paper. That way folks wouldn't have to walk down to your office every time they wanted to see it. They could all have their own copy."

Henderson looked profoundly embarrassed. He backed up a step, and Madigan, sensing that the tide was starting to turn, bored in. "You'll run the story, won't you, Milt? I mean, hell, you're here, you might as well write it up. I think you could do a better job than I could, being more objective, and all that. But you got to run it, for sure. How you going to identify yourself? 'Editor?'

'Journalist?'" Madigan paused, feigning deep thought for a few seconds. "How about . . . 'vigilante?' That do it, Milt? Seems like a fair description of what's going on here. You ask me, we can get rid of 'storekeeper' and 'rancher' and 'vendor of fine spirits.' Save space for the caption then. You could just say 'Vigilantes, Clarion, Colorado Territory.' 'Course, you could come up with something fancier than that, it's just a suggestion, you understand."

Flannery sensed that he was losing control, and he tried to rally support before it fully eroded. "He's just trying to bluff you, don't you see that? Hell, he's scared, and he's trying to scare us. But it won't work. I ain't scared."

"Me neither." Larry Martin stepped out of the crowd. The gangling cowhand staggered a couple of steps, then stopped. He wavered like a reed in a shifting current as he tried to keep his balance.

"You sure, Larry? Hell, you're lucky to be alive as it is," Madigan said. "Lucky Rivera didn't plug you, like he did the other idiots who were trying to burn down his barn."

"I didn't . . . "

"Don't be shy, Larry, go on, admit it. You and Stan Fish and Merle Hardman and Dick Henning. Maybe you figure you owe Stan, is that it? You think you owe him? You think you got to get past me and string up a man because he defended himself, is that it? What are you going to do, shoot him? Hang him? Or will you just burn down the goddamned jail? Or was that just Stan's thing?"

"You better shut up, Madigan," Flannery said, moving in beside Martin. "You got no call to be makin' fun of a dead man like that."

"Stan Fish wouldn't *be* dead, if he didn't try to take the law into his own hands." Madigan ignored Flannery now, addressing himself instead to the rest of the mob. "Because that's what happens when a man won't let the law take its course. Somebody gets hurt. This morning it was Stan Fish. Who's it gonna be tonight? Bill Matlock? Harry Childress?"

Martin went for his gun then, and Madigan fired. Martin groaned and went down, his hands clapped over his thigh. Blood was seeping from between his fingers, and Madigan moved forward to stand over him. "Get him to Doc Clemmons. Then go on home, dammit. Go the hell home where you belong."

He backed up to let two men come forward and help the wounded man to his feet. Bill Matlock and Milt Henderson propped him up, but Martin couldn't put weight on the injured leg. Madigan glanced at the wound and sighed inwardly. It wasn't as bad as it could have been. The bullet had missed the bone, and as near as he could tell, it hadn't hit an artery, either.

Milt Henderson turned to the mob and spoke for the first time. "Dave's right. We're making fools of ourselves." Bill Matlock licked his lips, and looked at Madigan, his face trembling with embarrassment. The stink of whiskey gusted toward Madigan with Matlock's every breath.

"Dave, I . . ."

"Forget it, Bill. Just get him to the Doc and go home."

Matlock nodded.

Flannery made one last desperate attempt to swing the crowd back to his side. "See that, he shot somebody to protect that little greaser. That ain't right."

"Dan, shut up!" Henderson snapped. "Go home."

Madigan backed up a few more steps. He looked at Dalhousie, who winked. "It was touch and go there for a few minutes, Pete," he said.

Holding up two fingers a fraction of an inch apart, Pete said, "The match was about this far from the powder, Davey."

Madigan sighed. "Yeah, I guess it was. But we dodged a bullet."

"Better'n old Larry did, anyhow."

17

When the sun came up, Madigan opened the door and walked outside. It had been quiet all night, and he was getting edgy. He knew what Matt Fisher said about mobs and sundown, but the tension was getting to him. All night long, he had been straining to hear things that weren't there and misinterpreting things that were. When a dog barked, he'd reached for his gun. A cat howled, and he dropped a cup of coffee. His nerves had turned an ordinary night full of ordinary sounds into the prelude to a lynching.

And now, with the sun starting to pour into the streets of Clarion, he wanted it all to be over. He had a long day ahead of him. He knew that.

And if Matt Fisher didn't get back as soon as he hoped to, it could be another long night. He had new respect for Matt now, and decided that he wouldn't want the sheriff's job for all the horses in Colorado. He regretted, too, ever having been critical of Fisher.

Standing on the boardwalk, a Winchester crooked in one elbow, he wondered how a man could stand the incessant twitch of his nerves, the constant tension. One night had been more than enough for Madigan.

The street seemed preternaturally peaceful. He wondered whether it was simply the quiet, or the sanitizing effect of the rising light. Either way, he was grateful for the respite. He knew the day could hold its own difficulties, but a mob was not likely to be one of them. There remained, however, the question of the gunman of the night before. Since the man had been on foot, there was no way to know whether it had been the same man who had stolen his horses and twice tried to kill him, but the odds were in favor of it. That gunman, too, seemed to prefer the darkness, but if he was getting desperate, and the attempt on Rivera's life seemed to suggest that he was, then it was possible he would try again during daylight.

Far up the street, he could see lights in the houses on the hill, but as the sun washed over the buildings, the lights became less and less noticeable. Madigan went back inside and poured himself another cup of coffee, then came out again and sat on the bench. He kept the rifle on his lap, his finger curled through the trigger guard, holding the coffee in his left hand.

Pete Dalhousie was sleeping at the desk, his head cradled on his arms, snoring to beat the band. Madigan found the irregular snorts and wheezes somehow comforting. The sounds were the only evidence that he was not alone in his predicament. Sipping the coffee, he wondered what would become of him. If he got a chance, he wanted to talk to Lou Cartwright at the bank, and hoped that the news would be good, although he was too much of a realist to think so.

At six thirty, the coffee gone, he stood up, held the Winchester in one hand, and stretched. He raised his arms high overhead and stood on tiptoe, suppressing a yawn as long as he could, then finally giving in to it. He rubbed his cheeks, feeling the whiskery stubble, and turned to look at his reflection in the smeary window behind him.

He looked like a saddle tramp. His eyes looked sunken, and the smattering of bristles gave his cheeks a dusty aspect, as if he hadn't washed for a few days. He felt tired and dirty, and more than a little depressed. More coffee wasn't the answer, but it was the best he could muster, and he went back inside, took the coffeepot from the stove, and poured himself another cup. Pete stirred, but did not wake, and Madigan went back outside.

At seven o'clock, he saw a man walking down the hill, and watched him approach. Dressed in a suit, letting his hands play with the shrubs, the man seemed to be in no hurry. He was still too far away for Madigan to recognize him. The man bent over to cup a blossom of some sort in his hand and sniff. For a moment, Madigan imagined a tweedy bee, and the thought made him smile.

When the man reached the bottom of the hill, he spotted Madigan and seemed to hesitate for moment, starting to cross the street, his steps stuttering and uncertain. Then he stopped, changed course again, and put his head down to plow straight on toward the temporary lawman. As he reached the boardwalk at the end of the next block, Madigan recognized him at last. It was Milt Henderson, the editor of the *Clarion*.

Feet tattooing the boards, Henderson tried to affect a determined strut, but traces of his earlier uncertainty dispelled the desired impression. He reached the break in the boardwalk, stepped down and stopped at the mouth of the alleyway running alongside the jailhouse.

"Morning, Milt," Madigan said.

"Dave. How are you?"

"Fine, yourself?"

Henderson wriggled his lips as if trying to dislodge something trapped between them and his gums, then a bulge showed where he ran his tongue along his teeth. Finally, he stepped up onto the boardwalk. He looked a little the worse for wear. A couple of patches of salt and pepper whiskers dappled his cheeks, and his eyes were a little bleary, their lids rimmed in red.

He swallowed hard, and said, "I'm really grateful to you, Dave."

"For what?" Madigan asked.

"For . . . well, I guess I made a fool of myself last night."

Madigan grinned. "You weren't alone, Milt. I'd like to say you were in good company, and I guess for the most part you were, but . . . "

"I've never done anything like that in my life. And I swear to God, I never will again. I don't know what got into me."

"Same thing that got into everybody else, I reckon. You're angry, and you had a little too much to drink. It isn't hard to let somebody talk you into making a jackass of yourself under those circumstances."

"If you and Pete hadn't been here, I don't know what would have happened."

"If me and Pete weren't here, Matty Fisher would have been. I don't imagine things would have turned out any different. Not much, anyhow. Maybe Larry Martin wouldn't be walkin' on a gimpy leg today, but otherwise I expect things would have turned out about the same as they did. I guess being an amateur, I made a few mistakes, and Martin'll limp a while because of it."

"You did fine. A lot better than we did."

"Well, it's ancient history, Milt. I just wish this whole thing were over."

"You really don't think Rivera did anything, do you?"

Madigan shook his head. "No, I don't Milt. I

don't have the faintest idea who did, but I know it wasn't Rivera, sure as I'm standing here. You know, before you fellows showed up, somebody else tried to shoot him through the jailhouse window. At least I hope it was somebody else. I hate to think the sonofabitch was standing right there in front of me, surrounded by friends and neighbors."

"I can't believe that's the case. I knew everybody in that crowd last night. I just don't believe one of them could be responsible."

Madigan shrugged. "Me either, but *somebody* took a shot at Rivera."

Henderson took a deep breath. "Well, I have to be getting to the office. Maybe I'll stop by later."

"I'll be here. At least until Matt gets back. Once that happens, it'll be a cold day in hell before I put on a badge again." Unconsciously, he reached up to pat the metal star on his shirt pocket. It felt cold to the touch, and he glanced down at it.

"It looks good on you, Dave," Henderson said. He tried to smile, but his facial muscles refused to cooperate, and fashioned themselves into something between a grimace and a wince.

Madigan thought about teasing him, but it was obvious that Henderson was embarrassed enough without teasing, so he said nothing.

Henderson moved on past, and as he walked along the boardwalk, his feet not quite finding a regular rhythm, he weaved the least little bit, and Madigan grinned in spite of himself.

He sat back down and finished his coffee,

watching the town slowly come alive. Shop doors opened, their glass panels sometimes catching the sun and sending spears of light lancing along the street. Windows were opened, the sashes rattling, the counterweights thumping a few times. Nearby, he could hear the hiss of cloth and the clatter of rings as curtains were pulled aside to let in the morning.

Far up the street, he saw Bill Matlock on the boardwalk, vigorously working a broom. A cloud of dust swirled out into the street and hung there like gunsmoke for several seconds before sifting to the ground.

The tattoo of hooves started as horses moved past, and the first wagon arrived, its boards creaking and groaning as the big wheels rocked through ruts baked into the dirt street. It was what morning was supposed to be like, Madigan thought. Folks going about their business, minding their own, leading quiet lives. It was such a jarring contrast with the night before that it seemed almost artificial, as if it were staged by some travelling showpeople.

Madigan found himself wondering about the ugliness of the night before, whether it was something that was always there, like a dark undercurrent, or if it had come from someplace else, spilling into Clarion like a poison that, given enough time, the sun and rain would leach away, leaving the town as peaceful and unsullied as it seemed, and wanted, to be.

At seven thirty, he went back inside, set the

cup on a small table beside the stove, and watched Pete shift uncomfortably on his arms once more, then sit bolt upright, as abruptly as if someone had stuck him with a hatpin.

"What time is it?" Dalhousie asked.

"Half past seven, Pete."

"Jesus, I didn't think I'd sleep so long. You shoulda woke me up, Davey."

"No need."

"Anything happening?"

Madigan shook his head. "Nothing at all. I saw Milt Henderson a little while ago."

"Bet he still had egg on his face, didn't he? Sumbitch made a fool out of hisself last night."

"He's a bit hung over, I think."

Pete laughed. "I'll bet he is. See, it's just like I was telling you, they get a little whiskey under their belts, and they forget who they are. Sometimes I think that's *why* they do it. I think they *want* to forget who they are, do something a little different. And all that's sittin' there inside them, waitin' for some loudmouth like Dan Flannery to whip it up. It's like pokin' a hornet's nest with a stick, boy. And when them hornets come pourin' out, you better run like hell, 'cause they'll sting anything they see."

"Well, I think the worst is over."

"Sure as hell hope so, Dave. Matt will be back tonight, anyhow, so you're off the hook by then." Pete yawned, stretched, and got up to pour himself some coffee. After a sip, he said, "Why don't you go get some sleep. Things are pretty quiet, and they should stay that way. I'll wake you if I need you."

"You sure?"

Pete nodded. "Yep, I'm sure."

Madigan walked to the door of the spare room. Rivera was fast asleep, wrapped in the blue blanket, one arm covering his eyes as he lay on his back. Madigan closed the door, and walked to the entrance to the cell-block.

He entered a cell and lay down on the bunk, closing his eyes, convinced that he was not going to sleep. Two hours later, someone shook him, and he bolted up to see Sarah grinning at him.

"What are you doing here?" he asked.

"Just wanted to give you the good news."

Madigan sat up, rubbing his yes. "What good news is that?"

"I saw Mr. Cartwright a little while ago . . . "

"And . . . ?"

". . . and he says he'll give us two extra weeks."

"I don't believe it!"

"It's true. He said Matt Fisher told him what was going on, and that he'd damn well better cooperate."

"Jesus, that's wonderful. Now, if only we get an extension from Fletcher . . . "

"We will. I just know it." She leaned over and kissed him on the head. "Go back to sleep. I just wanted you to know. Figured it was better for your dreams."

"It'll help," Madigan agreed.

"You coming home tonight?"

"I sure as hell hope so."

18

It was almost sundown when Pete shook Madigan awake. "Come on, Davey boy, time to get up," he said. He was entirely too cheery for Madigan's liking, but he sat up anyway, and scowled at Dalhousie.

"What's going on?" he asked.

"Matty's back."

That brought Madigan fully awake. "Already?"

"Hell, he looks like he been run over by a herd of buffalo, but he sure as hell is here. Come on, he wants to talk to you. He's in the office."

Madigan stood up and rubbed his eyes. Pete left the cell, and hung in the office doorway, waving his arm to hurry Madigan along. He could hear the sheriff talking to somebody, and walked out of the cell as Pete, satisfied that he was coming, disappeared through the doorway.

Fisher indeed looked worn out. His clothes were dusty, and his cheeks sagged. He was sitting at his desk, talking to Francisco Rivera, and glanced at Madigan for a moment, his red eyes wide with the effort to keep them open. He slugged down some coffee, then finished what he was saying. "So, you go on home, Señor Rivera. You go on home, and don't worry about anything. It'll be fine, I promise."

Rivera looked at Madigan, his face torn between confusion and relief. He tried to smile, but didn't quite pull it off, then walked to the peg rack and took down his gunbelt. Strapping it on, he said, "Thank you, Señor Fisher."

The sheriff nodded. "Don't mention it. I ain't doin' you a favor, I'm only doin' what's right." He stood up, took Rivera's rifle from the rack, and handed it to him. "You watch yourself, now, until we can figure this all out, you here?"

Rivera nodded.

"Your horse is up at Laverty's Livery. Pete'll go with you, and tell Liam it's all right for you to have it." He nodded at Dalhousie, and said, "You go on, Pete, then get your butt back here pronto. We still got some work to do."

The two men left the office, Rivera walking as if his feet didn't quite reach the ground, and Fisher turned to Madigan. "I got you a few extra days, Davey. Fletcher didn't like it, but Colonel Winslow twisted his arm."

Madigan broke into a broad grin. Grabbing Fisher's hand, he shook it vigorously, and said, "I don't know how to thank you, Matt."

"You'll thank me tonight, unless I miss my guess."

"Tonight?"

Fisher nodded. "Get some coffee, we got someplace to go, soon as Pete gets back."

"Where?"

"Señor Rivera's place."

"But I thought you said . . . "

"I know what I said. But I know something you don't, and I want to be there as soon as possible. Fact is, I want to be right on his tail all the way home, so drink your damn coffee and get moving. Pete's bringin' your horse when he comes back from Laverty's."

Madigan poured a cup of coffee, feeling as if his life were one endless flood of black liquid. Fisher stretched and stood up, and while Madigan sipped, the sheriff got a box of ammunition from the drawer under the gun rack.

"You ready?" he asked.

Madigan nodded. "Confused, but ready."

"Let's go, then." Fisher led the way out of the office, pulling the door closed behind him and not bothering to lock it. Up the street, they saw a dark figure riding toward them, another horse in tow. "That's Pete," Fisher said, as he climbed into the saddle. "Run on down there and mount up, Davey, we're in a hurry."

Madigan sprinted up the street, his legs tired

and stiff. He met Pete half a block from the office and took the sorrel's reins. As he swung into the saddle, he asked, "You know where we're going, Pete?"

Dalhousie shook his head. "Nope. But when Matty says go, I go. He knows what he's doin' Davey, so just come along for the ride. It'll all sort itself out."

Fisher rode up, reined in, and asked, "Rivera on the way home?"

Pete nodded. "Yep."

"You tell Liam what I want him to do?"

Again, Pete nodded. "He thinks you're crazy, but he said he'll do it."

"Let's move, then." Fisher spurred his mount, and the horse spurted forward, leaving Pete and Madigan to wheel around and break into a gallop after him.

They were riding hard, too hard for conversation, and Madigan found himself more confused than ever. Fisher shouted to his two deputies. "Keep a sharp eye peeled. I don't want Rivera to know we're right behind him."

"Matt, what are we doing?" Madigan shouted back.

"No time to talk now, Davey. Just hold your water."

Ten minutes later, Fisher slowed them. It was too dark to see very far ahead, and he was afraid the sound of the horses would spook Rivera, so he said, "Look, we'll just trot from here on. We'll get there in plenty of time."

By now, Madigan knew not to bother asking questions. It was another twenty minutes to Rivera's place, and when they broke over the last ridge, Madigan could see lights in the windows, but virtually nothing else. It looked as if the valley were inhabited by a small cluster of oblong fireflies.

"Let's get down close, as soon as we're sure he's inside," Fisher said. They sat there, watching the house for several minutes. Finally, a man on horseback passed in front of the windows, and Fisher said, "There he is."

A moment later, a larger block of light appeared as the front door opened. They could see Rivera entering the house, then the door closed and the large oblong disappeared.

"Okay," Fisher said. "Let's get down close. I want to be behind the house soon as we can. When we get to the bottom of the hill, we'll tie up the horses then find cover. Got it?"

He didn't wait for an answer, spurring his gray and heading down the first of several switchbacks. Madigan was right behind him, Pete bringing up the rear.

When they reached the bottom of the hills, Fisher pointed. "Over in them trees, that's where we'll leave the horses." He headed for a stand of lodgepoles, and dismounted, pulling his horse in among the trees and breaking through some stunted brush, dragging the horse behind him, then tying it off. Madigan tugged the sorrel through the brush and knotted its reins around a stunted pine that was all dead needles and prickly branches. When Pete had tethered his horse, Fisher said, "All right, now, bring your rifles, and look sharp."

The sheriff led the way, following the line of trees, keeping to the shadows, but picking a clear path to make the best time. They circled around behind the tiny cabin, and squatted down in the trees.

"You ready to tell me what the hell we're waiting for, Matt?" Madigan asked.

"We're waiting for the man who tried to shoot your lights out, Davey," Fisher grunted. "And unless I'm way off, he'll be here soon."

"How in the hell do you know that?"

"Because I had Liam Laverty pass the word that our little Mexican friend told me a few things, and as soon as that word gets around, which it will right quick, the man we want will come knocking on Rivera's door. Only he won't be paying a friendly visit. Now hush up."

The time dragged. It was getting chilly with the sun down, and Madigan didn't have a jacket. His teeth chattered a little, and Pete leaned over to say, "Christ, Davey, you keep up that racket, and you'll wake the damn dead."

"Hush up, Pete," Fisher snapped. "You just keep your eyes on that road. You see anything, you let me know." Pete had a pair of binoculars draped around his neck, and he trained them on the hillside, twiddling the knob as he tried to bring the shadow-wrapped road into focus.

Fisher stood up to stretch, and he yawned. "When this is all over, I'm gonna sleep till Christmas."

Madigan laughed. "I understand you twisted Lou Cartwright's arm for me, Matt. Thanks."

Fisher shrugged. "Don't mention it. I just . . . "

"I see something," Pete hissed. "Two men, halfway down the hill."

Fisher reached for the binoculars. "Give me them damn glasses," he said, snatching at them and jerking the strap over Pete's head. He raised them to his eyes, adjusted the focus, and whispered, "Damn!" He let the glasses drop to his chest. "Let's get ready to move. I don't want to cut this too close, but I got to let them make the first move."

He levered home a round, and the deputies followed suit. Getting into a crouch, Fisher whispered, "Okay, now, let's move down, right behind the house. Watch them close, now."

He broke into a sprint, heading down a slight slope, then moving to one corner of the cabin. When Madigan reached the house, Fisher sent him to the other corner. "Stay out of sight, Davey. But as soon as they're on the porch, you move. If they don't come in close, we'll have to go get 'em."

They could hear the clop of hooves, muffled by the night and the grass. Fisher nodded, and Madigan sprinted across the back of the house, stopping at the corner and pressing himself flat against the rear wall.

Moving carefully, Madigan eased around the

corner and tiptoed toward the front of the cabin, ducking under an open window halfway along the wall. He could hear the horses still approaching, but didn't want to risk peeking around the corner.

The horses stopped moving, and he heard the squeak of saddle leather as the men dismounted. Dropping to the ground, he risked a peek, and saw the two men moving toward the cabin. They both carried rifles, and it didn't look as though they were going to knock.

One of them dropped to his knees, and raised his rifle. "There he is, by God," the man hissed. Before Madigan could do anything to stop him, the man aimed and fired.

The crack of the rifle echoed like a giant handclap from the hillside. Glass had broken, and Madigan heard someone inside the cabin scream. Then footsteps thudded on the cabin floor as another gunshot cracked, this time from the second intruder's weapon.

"That'll be enough, boys," Fisher shouted. Madigan saw the two gunmen freeze for a moment, then one of them brought his rifle around toward Fisher's corner of the cabin. Without thinking, Madigan aimed and fired. He heard someone groan, and one of the riflemen fell to the ground. The second gunman turned and started back toward his horse, but another rifle shot cracked, this time from the far end of the cabin, and Madigan saw the gunman freeze. Little more than a shadow, he seemed to be motionless, but as Madigan came out from behind the cabin, he realized the man was slowly turning.

Matt Fisher was sprinting across the grass now, and the gunman suddenly leaped to one side. A spurt of flame, followed instantly by the crack of a pistol, split the night, and Fisher fired again. The gunman doubled over, then dropped to his knees as Madigan closed on him. He heard the door of the cabin bang open, and Fisher shouted, "Rivera, it's all right. It's the sheriff. Just stay inside."

The two gunmen lay in the grass separated by a few yards. The one Madigan had hit lay on his side. Madigan knelt beside him, leaning close to get a clear look at him. He reached out to remove the man's hat, and saw Merle Hardman, his face a mask of pain. "Jesus Christ!" Madigan whispered.

He pulled Hardman's pistol from its holster, then retrieved the dropped rifle. Walking toward the second gunman, Madigan moved in beside the kneeling Fisher and looked over his shoulder. "My God," he blurted. "It's Dan Flannery . . . "

Fisher turned to look up at him. "Who the hell did you think it would be?"

"I . . . " But Madigan was speechless. For a moment, all he could do was shake his head. Finally, he found his voice again. "I had no idea."

"That's because you didn't know Flannery also bid on that Army horse contract. That's why I went to Peterson, to find out if anybody had a reason to want to see you fall on your face. And when I talked to Lou Cartwright before I left town, he told me that Flannery had a note coming due in a couple months, and that he was gonna have trouble making the payment. Seems like old Dan wanted to do you in, Davey, to save his own ranch. I think if you check his horse, you'll find that horseshoe we been spotting all over the place. I kept seeing the tracks around town, and knew it had to be somebody right under our noses."

"But what did he have against Rivera?"

"He was setting him up to take the blame for you losin' horses, and for the shooting. But Stan Fish didn't handle the cow business any too well, and it was starting to come apart at the seams on him. He hired Stan and the others from Mitchell's crew to keep himself clear."

Madigan felt a hand on his shoulder, and turned to see Francisco Rivera grinning at him. Madigan tipped his hat back on his head and sighed. "Christ, maybe it'll work out after all. If I can get those horses to Fort Peterson on time."

"Señor, I will help you with the horses," Rivera said. "You helped me, and so I will help you. Then we will get *borracho* in the Arrowhead saloon, no?"

Madigan laughed. "With my luck, anything's possible, Francisco."

Bill Dugan is the pseudonym of a full-time writer who lives in upstate New York with his family.

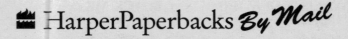